The Jinn

The Jinn

Mason Bushell

Chapeltown Books

British Library Cataloguing in Publication Data
A Record of this Publication is available from the British Library

ISBN 978-1-910542-62-0

This edition published 2020 by Chapeltown Books
Manchester, England

Cover illustration © Ashleigh James

Contents

The Talia and the Jinn

Enough was enough for Talia; she was done being the victim. She was done getting beaten and bullied every day. The cherry blonde sat cross-legged on her bed, wearing her nightdress. Her emerald eyes shone as she took in the effigy of a creature of myth. A terrifying horned creature of fire upon a talisman in her hand. The fire demon would make things right. Talia pressed the coin between her palms and uttered the summoning spell. At once her cool room became muggy warm. An orange hue came over the blue walls. Her computer screen blinked out, and the mouse crashed to the floor.

"You summoned me," said a booming voice, one that sounded quite fed-up. Talia looked about her room, seeing nobody. Shuffling along to her desk, she let her bare legs hang off the bed. They felt warm like the desk was on fire. "Well, what do you want me to do?" said the voice. This time Talia saw him. A figure whose mighty muscles appeared carved from granite. He was fiery orange, dripping in flames. Even his hair was aflame rather like a candle, with him being just five inches tall.

"I was expecting you to be taller, and more frightening."

"Huh, they all do, but nobody ever summons me right." The Jinn folded his arms and looked up to Talia, sitting like a giant before him. "You must do the spell when you're angry, and with destruction in mind, if you want the demon to come and burn your bloody house down."

"Sorry, I didn't know. I hoped you could go to my school and take care of those who bully me." Talia sighed. "But you're too small."

"Really." The Jinn unfolded an arm and pointed it at her. At once she squealed as her nightdress burst into flames. She was forced to pull it off and stomp it out, revealing her bruised body.

"That was unnecessary, you're supposed to help me, not torch me." Talia padded to the wardrobe and pulled her dressing-gown on.

"Well, now you know I'm diminutive in size but not power." The Jinn began pacing, his footsteps causing the desk to smoke as he moved. "So, let me get this straight. You want me to go to your school and what, burn it down with the bullies inside?"

"No, I wanted you to find those who hurt me, and burn their homework, punish them and teach them a lesson." Talia picked up her coffee and put it down at once – it was cold. The Jinn touched the mug, it was the same size as he was. Inside the brown liquid began to bubble and steam, leaving the girl smiling at him. "You still have uses though."

"Watch it, I'm not going to be your bloody butler."

"Touchy, aren't you?"

"Hundreds of years getting mis-summoned for stupid vendettas does that to a Jinn."

7

"So, you won't help me then?" Talia sipped her coffee, her eyes on the fiery figure now melting a rubber pig he was leaning on.

"I can't."

"Sure, you can, you burned my nightdress." Talia kicked the still smoking garment with her bare toes.

"Burning a bully's pants off won't make them stop hurting you." The pig suddenly collapsed pitching the Jinn off his feet. "Oh, I wish I could turn my flames off," he complained while getting up. Talia giggled at him.

"You're funny."

"I'll be on stage every night at the comedy club." The Jinn snorted and paced again. "Look bullies attack people because they're jealous of them, or because they're the weakest in class. You must figure out which and confront them."

"Charlie and Paulette are just horrible though. You saw my bruises."

"I did. I trust your tutors do nothing?"

"They give out detentions. Missing a lunch break never stops them. In fact, it makes them worse." Talia felt tears prickling her eyes. If the Jinn wouldn't help what more could she do?"

"Hey, no tears, that's not going to beat those bullies. I want you to go to school and catch Charlie and Paulette on their own. I want you to get in their faces and demand to know why they attack you. Let them see you're not scared, and that you're going to start swinging for them if they don't quit. That should stop them."

"If it doesn't, then what Jinn?"

"Well." The Jinn smiled at her. "If it doesn't, I'll go and torch their homework and burn their pants off."

The Talia and the Jinn 2

Talia once again sat on her bed wearing her new nightdress. The Jinn had torched her old one when she summoned him last night. His advice hadn't worked either, the bullies were worse today. She picked up the talisman and looked at the horned creature of fire upon it. She hoped he'd keep his word. With a hopeful sigh, she said the incantation. In moments, her room grew orange and muggy warm around her.

"Yes," boomed the Jinn's voice from atop the wardrobe, "you summoned me. What do you want?" he said, picking at his fingers as he leaned against a stray nail. Talia gasped at the five-inch tall man. His muscles appeared carved from granite and dripping in flames.

"Jinn, what are you doing? Get down before you incinerate my wardrobe! My mother nearly killed me for the pig you destroyed yesterday."

"Oh, it's you again." The Jinn blinked out of existence, reappearing on Talia's saucer of biscuits. "Sorry about the pig. I trust my wisdom failed."

"Big time." Talia indicated her black eye with sadness consuming her. "They said they weren't jealous and started pummelling me again."

"I see." The Jinn smoothed a hand through his flaming hair. The chocolate melting off the biscuit beside him. "Did you fight back?"

"No." Talia shook her head.

"Why? You heard the phrase slap-happy, right?"

"So?"

"So, it's for this situation. You slap the bullies, you feel happy." The Jinn took a bow.

"No, I slap bullies, I get expelled, and killed by my mother."

"Expelled? Huh. I've been expelled from dimensions more times than I can count for standing up for myself. I always marched right back through the portal and won the next round."

"How?"

"You'll be surprised what burned sausages and balls of fire can achieve." The Jinn raised his smouldering eyebrows and smirked. "So, will you give those bullies a flame grilling tomorrow?"

"No, they'll just beat me even more." Talia flopped back on the bed, a defeated figure. The Jinn kicked free of the pool of chocolate he was standing in and flew into the air above her.

"Not if I bring the flames, they won't," he said, leaving her smiling.

The following lunchtime, Talia walked from the school building on to the playing field. She looked pretty in her uniform of emerald green skirt and blazer over a white blouse, and tie. The only part she liked was her plaited pigtails, as her mother had specially put them in for her this morning. She sat upon a bench with her cheese rolls, near a telephone mast. She wanted to watch the footballers on the field, while she ate. Trouble soon came her way, it always did.

"Ah, there's Ta-Ta, Charlie" jeered an overweight girl.

"Yeah, shall we rip her pigtails off, Paulette?" asked her friend with folded arms. Talia ignored them and made to bite into her roll. Charlie snatched it away and stomped it into the grass. Paulette picked up the other with a fat hand and took a big bite.

"Oh, you'll pay for that," Talia said with a fire in her eyes. Paulette snatched her right pigtail and forced her to stand.

"Go on then, make me pay," she said through her mouthful.

"You asked for it." Talia squeezed the talisman, saying the incantation in her mind. Only she felt the temperature rising, just a little.

"Well go on then, do something." Charlie put her hand in Talia's bag and shrieked. Withdrawing it, she revealed all the hairs were singed, her false nails had melted, and her signet ring was smoking.

"Naughty girl, that's not your bag," said a voice.

"Nice trick." Charlie threw Talia to the ground. "Make her pay, Paulette."

"My pleasure." The big girl stood astride the fallen student and made to grab her by the blazer. Talia looked at her with a fearless stare and folded her arms.

"My pleasure too." The voice came from the muggy ether. The weighty bully looked about her in confusion. "You're rather sparky for a bully, Paulette. Shame it's causing an inferno in your rucksack."

"What?"

"Paulette, your bag's smoking," Charlie cried. Paulette threw it off and watched flames engulf it in a small blaze.

"No! My homework. Miss Childers will kill me," she cried. Talia stood and grinned.

"Shame your homework wasn't on combustion," she said.

"It's all coals on a bonfire now," the voice broke into laughter. Charlie was scared, she backed away and sat on the bench, shaking with fear. Paulette, on the other hand, was seething.

"You did this."

"How? I was lying on the grass remember?"

"You did it."

"Liar." Talia grinned.

"You burned her hand." Paulette grabbed her pigtails.

"Liar."

"You burned my homework."

"Pants on fire." Talia broke free and watched the bully's eyes grow wide. Her backside was getting very warm, very quickly. She screamed and began running across the field with her hand clutched beneath her smoking skirt. Everybody watched and stood

13

laughing at her as she ran across the football pitch. Flames burst forth from her crotch, and she jumped into the pond, creating a lot of steam.

"Talia, what's going on? How did you do that?" Charlie asked.

"Never you mind. Just promise to leave me alone, and it won't happen again."

"Deal. I'm sorry for bullying you." Charlie put out a hand, and Talia shook it. The bully looked frightened as she walked toward Paulette in the pond. It was then Talia looked to the aluminium phone mast and smiled. The Jinn sat on the top, pretending to file his nails.

"Thank you," she said.

"I haven't had this much fun since the seventies."

"Really, what happened in the seventies?"

"Oh yeah, I loved Disco Inferno." The Jinn began dancing on the pole.

Talia chuckled at him. "Well, I'm glad you had fun, I appreciate your help."

"My pleasure, Talia. I told you I'd set their pants on fire, didn't I?"

"You did. That was hilarious." Talia laughed again. "Oh Jinn, I command you to be free of the fire, and to be the wielder of all the powers you need to help good people."

"Yahoo!" The Jinn performed a somersault and snapped his fingers putting his flames out. "Thank you for freeing me, dear lady, I'm forever indebted to you. It's time for me to party." The Jinn clicked his fingers and vanished into the air, leaving disembodied laughter in his wake.

A large ham and cheese baguette appeared in Talia's hands, and she sat to eat. She wouldn't need the Jinn anymore. The bullies wouldn't dare touch her again. At least if they wanted to keep their pants from combusting, anyway!

The Jinn and the Dog

A perfect summer's afternoon for a barbecue, at least Andrew's family thought so. A typical scenario, everybody wanted something, but nobody actually wanted to help make it happen. Nevertheless, it was nice standing in the sun while setting coals in the tray of the barbecue. With that done, Andrew put a quick-light charcoal bag on the coals and took out his gas lighter. It was then Fred, the black Labrador, climbed from the sun lounger and hid underneath it. The garden was filled with clicking noises, then swearing as the lighter refused to ignite the bag.

"Bloody things never work. Come on spark, you useless, mechanical, piece of crap," Andrew complained while still pressing and clicking away at the device. Within five minutes, frustration overtook him, the lighter went flying over the sun lounger and disappeared into the hedge.

"Woof," barked Fred running after it. He came back and sat before his master with the lighter in his mouth. Andrew had taken a coin from his pocket. He'd found it in the park that morning with a hair clip bearing the name *Talia*. It depicted a horned creature surrounded by fire and the words of an ancient incantation.

"Good boy, Fred. I need this flaming guy to get the bloody barbecue lit, I think." Taking the lighter from Fred, he handed him a biscuit and smoothed his head for a moment. Fred retreated to the sun lounger to enjoy his biscuit. Andrew held the coin and read the incantation. "You won't help demon, I better go and find some matches." Chuckling to himself he added, "Stupid thing" on his way indoors. Never did he realise that the coin was a talisman. He didn't even notice the air growing warmer, and the darkness beneath the sunbed turn orange.

"Yes? You summoned me?" The Jinn walked to the edge of the sun lounger and peered out with a sigh.

"What do you want?" he asked. The Jinn stood only five-inches tall and had muscles that looked carved from granite. Thanks to Talia, he was no longer dripping in flames. Sure, he could still conjure them, but she'd freed him of their curse. Now he stood wearing Bermuda shorts and sunglasses. Something he could never do before. Hearing some thumping about above him, he looked for the cause. He found the largest, blackest pair of nostrils he'd ever seen, hovering a centimetre from his head. They sniffed so vigorously that they sucked his flame ginger hair right inside the enormous nose. The Jinn pressed his hands against the wet, rubbery snout and pulled himself free.

"Marvellous. I get summoned by nobody, and then rewarded by a doggy snot shampoo. Just bloody marvellous," he grumbled.

"Sorry about that, old chap," said the dog. Had

Andrew been outside, he'd have heard the dog whine instead of hearing the words.

"Don't mention—" A loud sucking sound cut the Jinn off. All he saw was a massive pink tongue shoot out of the dog's mouth. It slapped him off his feet as it licked him from head to foot. The Jinn picked himself up, dripping wet with saliva. "If you kiss me again, I'm going to turn your tongue into bacon and use your teeth as piano keys got that?"

"I'm a dog, I like licking things. What do you expect?" Fred climbed from the sun lounger and sat on the grass, his nose a centimetre above the Jinn. "What are you?" he asked.

"I'm a Jinn." The little man conjured some heat to dry himself off. "Here eat this." Summoning a white lozenge-shaped thing, he held it aloft.

"Why?" asked the dog.

"It's a mint sweet. Your breath smells like a horse's backside."

"Okay sorry." The dog reached down with its jaws open and closed them on the mint. The Jinn yelped.

"Bloody hell, dog. Watch what you bite, will you." The Jinn rubbed his squashed fingers. Above him, the dog crunched the mint and swallowed it.

"You're mighty stroppy for a little man, aren't you?" he said.

"So, would you be. I mean, you didn't summon me, then you near sucked me into your nasal passages before half-drowning me with one hell of a

French-kiss. I'm having a bad day." The Jinn leant against the sun lounger with a sigh.

"French kiss, hey." The dog paused to scratch himself, showering the Jinn with loose hairs. "You should see what my pack leader's—"

"Hell no! I do not want to know about the bedroom exploits of your humans, thank you very – bloody – much." The Jinn brushed himself down. "And watch where you're flinging your fur too. You're damned lucky you're not a fleabag."

"Hey, who you calling a fleabag? I'll have you know that I bathe regularly." The dog lay down, setting his paws either side of the Jinn.

"Good. I don't suppose you know why I was summoned do you?"

"I think my master was trying to make flames come out of that metal thing. When he does, sausages usually fall out of it for me to eat." The dog licked his lips. "I like sausages."

"No doubt. I wouldn't stay in this garden if I were you."

"Why's that, Jinn?"

"When humans can't set fire to something, they're so dumb that they resort to dangerous methods, and boom!" The Jinn raised his eyebrows.

"Right. When he comes out, I'm going indoors." The dog looked toward the house. The sound of utensils bashing about could be heard inside. "So, you grant wishes, do you?"

"Something like that. You want something?"

"A nice big bone would be great." The dog looked hopeful.

"Consider it done." The Jinn winked.

Andrew had finally found some matches. Walking out into the garden he was hit by something so big and heavy that it knocked him flat.

"Where in Madam Wiffen's bloomers did that come from?" Andrew sat up holding his head. Across his stomach was a tyrannosaurus leg bone. "I must be going mad." Kicking the bone off him, he watched a pleased looking Fred clamp his jaws on and drag the bone across the lawn. "Even you can't manage a bone that big, old fellow." Andrew looked about him on the way to the barbecue. There were no planes in the blue sky and no rational explanations for the bone. Dismissing it, he struck a match and held it to the quick-light bag. It didn't ignite, the match went out.

"Darling, hurry up with the barbecue. We're hungry," said his wife by the patio doors.

"Bloody barbecue." Andrew failed to light it with four more matches. "Alright, dear," he said before marching around the house.

The Jinn stood leaning on the leg of the sun lounger again. His eyes grew wide when the human man returned. He was holding a big red can with the word 'petrol' in white letters upon it. Even as he took flight, the Jinn saw him shaking some of the fuel into the bottom of the barbecue.

"You summoned me, and I must tell you not to do that," he said. His voice booming around the garden.

Andrew looked about him, seeing nothing and nobody. Shaking his head, he opened the matchbox again.

"Okay, barbecue, time to cook me some burgers, and fast."

"If you light that match, you're going to cook the whole bloody garden in a microsecond," warned the Jinn landing on the table beside the man. Andrew looked right at him, blinked a few times and refocused on the task at hand.

"Little man in Bermuda shorts, the heat must be making me mad," he mumbled. Striking the match, he heard a whoomph and then his world went – BANG!

The barbecue blew apart like an incendiary grenade. The lawn and hedges burst into flames as the quick-light bag flew over the neighbour's like a stray comet. The sun lounger flipped over and Fred the dog streaked indoors. His last view was of the Jinn sailing through the hedge with his boxer shorts on fire.

In the midst of his burning garden, Andrew climbed, choking and coughing, to his feet, his clothes and hair smoking, and he looked brassed off.

"Tammy, dear, I've come to a decision," he said.

"Yeah, what's that?" she replied without coming outside.

"Bugger the barbecue, let's go to MacDonald's."

"Good idea, you bloody idiot." The Jinn landed in a pile of leaf litter amid the bushes. At once, he slapped the flames out of his Bermuda shorts. "It's supposed to be me setting people's pants on fire, not you." Standing, he looked straight into the eyes of a toad.

"Croak... Bad day, friend?... Croak," it said. The Jinn looked daggers at it.

"You hush and hop it."

The Jinn looked back to the fiery garden. "Well Fred, I told you so," he said before disappearing back from whence he came.

The Governor and the Jinn

He was known as 'Dominator' Doug. He was the Governor around these parts, although that position had come under threat of late. Sitting in his sweatbox of an office above the warehouse, Doug knew he was running out of time and needed a plan. A knock on the door made him groan; some peace and quiet would have been nice too.

"Yeah, what yer want?" he called in a gravelly voice.

"It's us, Guv," answered a man coming in.

"Ah, Jonesy, Slick an' Ton, what yer got to tell me?" Doug knitted his fingers on the desk before him, showing a thick gold ring on his finger.

"The Colts are coming, Guv." Ton pounded his large fist into his hand. "Can we smash 'em?"

"Yeah, let us kill some of 'em to show we mean business." Slick leant against the wall and flicked a coin into the air.

"What's that you got there?" Doug put out a hand.

"Just a coin, Guv." Slick handed to him. To defy him was never a wise move.

Doug saw the features of a horned demon surrounded with fire upon the coin. "Well, this is right nice. Must be worth some decent nicker, I bet. Don't mind if I keep it, do yer?" he said.

"Nah, it's yours, Guv." Slick looked sad at the loss of his coin. "What about the bloody Colts."

"You lot, go down them stairs and make sure they can't get on the premises, alright."

"We want guns," requested Jonesy.

"Yeah, guns, Guv," agreed Ton looking like a murderous bulldog.

"Let me see to that. You just buy me time, alright. Now get out, the lot a yer." Doug pointed to the door.

Once he was alone, he took up the coin. Could it buy him a few guns? It sure looked valuable. He read the incantation etched around the demon, then thrust it on the desk. Taking a picture on his phone, he used the image search function and learned it was a talisman. It had barely registered when the room grew hot and took on an orange glow.

"You sum— Ah – Ah – Achoo!" The sneeze was so violent that it sent warehouse paperwork billowing across the room. "Bloody hell. When was the last time you dusted this place?"

"Who's there? Come out where I can see yer." Doug rose with a sizeable combat knife in his hand. "I never dust my office. I'm the governor, not the bloody maid."

"I'm up here, and you summoned me, you lazy git." The Jinn stepped around a cardboard box. At five inches tall it was bigger than him. The granite-like little man was naked save for his khaki shorts and red sunglasses in his fiery ginger hair. "Now, put that knife down, before you cut yourself, you bloody idiot."

"Oi, I told you, I'm the governor around here. Not you, get it?"

"Well, you summoned me. So, shut up, and govern me. I want to get back to my relaxation if you don't mind." The Jinn folded his arms and looked expectant.

"You're a genie, are you?" Doug saw the little man nod and sneered. "Yeah, good. I want guns, big guns."

"Guns? What do you want guns for?"

"I want my fellas to blow some ugly faces off. Yer know? To show them Colts who's in charge around here." Doug sneered and chuckled at the thought.

"Oh, brother." The Jinn slapped a hand to his face. "Six-thousand-years humans have been on this planet, and still they want to walk around blowing people's faces off like it's a gentlemanly sport or something." The Jinn put on a feminine voice. "Come on kids, let's go out and blow our neighbours' faces off. That will be really fun won't it, boys?"

"Think yer funny, do yer?" Doug wiped his nose with a forearm, his smile gone.

"You'd think, that by now some of you brainless morons would have learned about a nice friendly bit of diplomacy."

"Bugger diplomacy, they want to kill me. Can yer

get me guns, or what?" Doug stepped around his desk and approached the Jinn. The little man looked up to him and shrugged.

"Sure, you want some C4, so you can blow their balls into orbit, too?" The Jinn rolled his eyes.

"Yeah, good idea."

"Huh, your boys would probably blow this building up with them still inside it. You want to end up wearing your warehouse rather than working in it, do you?"

"Shut up, and get me the goods."

"Fine." The Jinn shook his head then snapped his fingers. A large crate appeared in mid-air, hovered for a second, then crashed down flattening the desk and destroying the computer monitor in a shower of sparks. "Bugger, sorry about that." The Jinn looked sheepish for a moment.

"That's alright, just fix it."

"Will do." The Jinn gestured, making the box move aside. Then repaired the desk with further hand movements.

"Nice." Doug went to the door. "Fellas, get up here, now."

One-hour later Doug and his men stood at the warehouse gates, each man armed with a large and deadly M4 Carbine machine gun. Beyond the gates stood twelve leather jacket-wearing Colts. Their boss

(Biceps) Billy stood before them flexing his large arms with a menace about him. "Hey Dominator, ready to give me your land, or your life?"

"Gent bent, Biceps. One step closer and we'll blow yer faces off." Doug beckoned him forward. He wanted to fight, to end this while he had the weapons to succeed.

"You sure, you can do that? Those incompetent fools probably don't even know where the triggers are."

"Shut yer face and come get some then." Doug smacked his chest with aggression.

"Huh, really. Old Slicky there probably couldn't shoot the broad side of a bank van, if he were an inch away from it." Biceps laughed showing his yellowed teeth.

"That's it. Let me blow him away, Guv," Slick bristled as he clicked the safety off his gun.

"That's what he wants. Just hold yer temper." Doug faced Biceps. "This land has belonged to me and my fellas for decades. What gives you the right to take it from me?"

"Simple. You ain't got the balls to stop me."

"That's it. Let em have it, boys." Doug pointed forward and crouched as his men clicked their carbines into action, unleashing a cloud of bubbles upon their opponents.

"What the hell is this, Dominator? You planning a foam party." Biceps laughed. "Colts, bring these losers to their knees." His signal had his men draw stiletto knives as they charged through the gates. The moment they crossed into the warehouse grounds it happened. Each man found himself holding a bunch of roses instead of his blade.

"Look out, boys, they'll bend their knees and propose, in a minute," Doug retorted as Ton seized two men and sent them flying into piles of pallets and crates with ease. "Go or Ton will destroy all your men with his bare hands."

"Retreat, Colts. You win this round, Dominator. However, we'll be back to end you." Biceps made a rude gesture and ran down the street, his men right behind him.

"And stay out," yelled Jonesy.

"Alright, fellas. Get inside. We'll have a toast to our victory." Doug made to follow. Instead, he saw the Jinn sat on a low roof, bubbles billowing from a pipe he was smoking. "I s'pose yer think that was funny?"

"I'm forever blowing bubbles," sang the Jinn.

"Shut yer face and give me real weapons next time, Jinn."

"Wasn't this better though, no deaths, no extreme violence. They even brought you roses." The Jinn floated down to stand on a pallet level with the mob boss. He was grinning from ear to ear, he'd had fun even if nobody else had.

"No, it bloody wasn't. When they come back, I

want bazookas, grenades, and miniguns. I command you to make it happen." Doug pointed a finger at the Jinn. "Don't cross me again, Jinn."

"Ugh, when was the last time you clean these fingernails. Looks like you have a rubbish tip under each one." The Jinn smiled, vanished and reappeared on the gate post. "Now do I want to be responsible for London becoming a crater when you boneheads go all apocalyptic?" he mused.

"Stop insulting me, and get me the weapons, Jinn."

"Nope, nope definitely not." The Jinn vanished leaving the words *Be diplomatic, you bloody idiot* sparkling in the air.

The Magician and the Jinn

"You're supposed to be Archie the Illusionist. Lately, you've become Archie the boring idiot." Jodie the stage manager stood hands on hips. Her lips pursed with annoyance.

Archie looked up at her from his seat on a magic box. He flipped an ace of diamonds over his fingers, waved his hand and made it vanish. "I'm doing the best I can." Archie let out a sigh and cursed as his deck of cards fell from his hand, scattering across the floor. "They used to love my act."

"Well, get a new act or get out of my theatre." Jodie stomped off leaving the magician a sagging figure behind the curtains. Surrounded by his magic props, he felt like a failure. He picked up a limp wand and slammed it into his magic hat. It was then footsteps announced a visitor.

"Hey, magic-man. What's a matter with you?"

"Hallo, Charlie. I'm done for mate. Nobody likes me anymore." Archie looked aloft to the brown eyes of the near seven-foot-tall stagehand. He'd come to sweep the stage and was leaning on his broom.

"Aw, well, I like you, Archie," he said.

"Thanks, mate. What I need right now is a miracle." Archie stood and began loading his tricks into his metamorphosis box.

"Here, my father Doug said this coin could bring me good luck. He said it taught him diplomacy and now his warehouse is stronger than ever. Maybe, it might help with your fortunes too." Charlie handed over a large silver coin bearing the image of a horned demon surrounded in flames.

"This is no coin, it's a talisman."

"Whatever, can you do a trick with it?" Charlie began pulling on a rope drawing the curtains aside and revealing the stage and empty seating.

"Maybe. Can I borrow this?"

"Keep it, mate."

"Thanks." Archie picked up the hat and walked from the backstage area to his dressing-room. A small space with white walls, no window, a clothes rail and a mirror back desk to prepare at. Sitting down, he tossed his top hat on the rack, then read the incantation before typing it into his phone to search for the coin. Around him, the room grew hot and orange. The top hat fell to the floor, dispensing the wand, and somebody groaned in pain.

"Cor, bloody hell. What happened," said a booming voice from the direction of the hat on the floor. Archie's eyes widened as he cautiously lifted the hat. He revealed a five-inches tall muscular man. He looked to have been carved from granite and was naked save from black leather shorts, and black sunglasses in his flame-red hair.

"Who – er – what are you?"

"Ahh, I suppose you think it's funny summoning me into a bloody hat." The Jinn stood rubbing his backside while looking up to Archie in his magician's cape. "You tall, insensitive git."

"Sorry, I didn't even know I could summon you." Archie felt stunned by the little man.

"Oh, you're one of those?" The Jinn picked up the limp wand, snapped his fingers and turned it into a stick of rock candy.

"One of what?" Archie watched him chewing on the enormous candy with interest.

"A wizard wannabe. A fake in a cape, an illusionist with sparks instead of spells. Bet you can't even disappear a coin, properly."

"Oh really?" Archie took up the talisman, holding it between finger and thumb. With a flourish, he vanished it. "There see."

"Huh, it's up your sleeve."

"No, it's naaaah!" Archie shot toward the ceiling and found himself hanging upside down in mid-air. The Jinn made hand gestures. "Agh, I'm not a bloody ragdoll, put me down." Archie felt himself shaking about, until the talisman dropped from his sleeve to the floor.

"See." The Jinn snapped his fingers. Archie fell onto his chair and thundered to the floor with a crash. The Jinn folded his arms with a smug look.

"That was unnecessary," he complained.

"Next time don't lie. You know I hate phoney magic people. I caught a witch out once. She flew off the handle and hurled her cauldron at me." The Jinn vanished and reappeared looking in the mirror.

"Then there was the wizard who couldn't do magic. He asked me how to deal with an angry druid that was bothering him."

"Did you help him?"

"Sure, I told him to deal with him very carefully." The Jinn grinned at his reflection. "So, now what do you want me to do?"

"I'm a complete failure." Archie took a matchbox, revealed it to be full, shut it, then opened it again. This time it was empty. "Nobody loves my tricks anymore."

"No wonder. Merlin was doing better tricks than that a thousand years ago. Every dinner time that wizard would magically glue a knife into the margarine block, he'd call it excali-butter. Only worthy diners could use the butter after that. The king was never amused. That bloody sword was his best trick."

"What about me. What can you do to help me?" Archie looked hopeful.

It was curtain time, the next evening.

"Ladies and Gentleman, I give you Archie the Illusionist," announced Jodie with a hopeful look at the stage. The curtains opened and the audience applauded, but Archie wasn't there. His usual illusions were in place, but the stage was devoid of life.

"Boo, we want magic."

"Yeah, Daddy said, there was magic here." A little girl jumped to her feet her face contorted, close to tears.

"You want magic, girl?" The voice had come from the ether, right by her side. "This is magic ladies and gentlemen." A fire erupted on centre stage, it burned into a boiling column. The crowd gasped as it exploded in a puff of smoke revealing the magician dressed in a white suit. "Sorry for the delay, I caught my trousers on fire during testing," he said leaving everybody laughing.

Spinning on the spot, he vanished and reappeared wearing all green.

"Now." He looked about the audience. "You sir come and join me."

"Me?" a man in his forties rose.

"Yes, you'll do. I can borrow him, can't I, madam?"

"He's my husband, do what you like with him. Just make sure he's back to do the washing up," she replied, getting a dirty look from her man.

"Thank you, madam." Archie guided the man into the spotlight on stage. He raised a hand, producing a deck of cards from thin air before fanning them out. "Pick one, and show the audience." The man did as he was told. "Good, put it back in the deck."

"So, you manipulated the deck to make my card easier to find, did you?"

"Oh, we have a smart arse in the house ladies and

gentleman." Archie never blinked, he raised the deck and watched it erupt into flames. "You sir, chose the Jack of Diamonds." The audience applauded.

"No, I did not." The man folded his arms. Archie held out a hand and conjured a large wand. Throwing it high, he caused it to become a large shawl. He spun it around the man covering his body. Then in a puff of smoke, the shawl and the man's trousers were gone. He was stood wearing huge white boxer shorts emblazoned with the Jack of Diamonds.

"A man's boxer shorts never lie. Ladies and gentleman." Archie bowed to his applause.

"Huh, nice trick." The man folded his arms. "Can I sit now?"

"One second." Archie took a tall cardboard box and lowered it over the man. Next, he took a sword and proceeded to slice the box into sections, getting lower and lower. The audience gasped for the man had vanished. Archie walked to his empty seat and laid a black cloak over it. With a flourish he flicked it skyward, revealing the man in his seat. The audience burst into fresh applause.

Archie did trick after trick until his time was done. Exhausted but smiling from ear to ear, he walked off stage. Jodie stood applauding him.

"You were amazing. Archie the Illusionist can do great magic after all," she said.

"I wouldn't bet on it." Archie snapped his fingers, engulfing himself in fire. It extinguished a second later revealing the Jinn hovering in mid-air. Jodie flinched back in shock. "Don't panic, woman. I'm not here to hurt you. That useless twit, Archie. Couldn't do a thing I told him to. He's been sitting on his arse in the dressing-room all night."

"Figures. I'm going to fire him, right now."

"Wait. It's you stressing him out that's causing the problem. He can't focus and do anything right for fear of getting fired." The Jinn saw the manager preparing to speak and held up a hand. "Don't open your mouth, just listen. Archie can do what I did, but only if you let him, only if you encourage him."

"Fine, teach him and I'll help." Jodie sighed and headed toward the dressing room with the Jinn at her shoulder.

The Baby and the Jinn

It wasn't the squirrel bounding among the branches who had ten-month-old baby Petey gurgling from the picnic blanket. In fact, he was watching the man in the white suit on the bench making coins vanish and reappear from the air.

"Time to go home, Petey darling," said his mother, Liza, lifting him from the blanket surrounded by a carpet of daisies on the park meadow. He smiled and took hold of a lock of her red hair. He was soon safely buckled into his pushchair. Liza paused at the bench to put her picnic rubbish in the bin. It was then the magician made a large silver coin appear. With a magical flourish it left his hand, and Petey found it in his. The baby looked to the mystical man, but he was gone before Petey's mother even noticed he was there. Petey put the coin in his mouth and made a funny face, it tasted awful. Liza pushed him home blissfully unaware of what her son was holding.

Soon Petey was seated in his playpen at home. Surrounded by his array of colourful toys and the cartoons on the tv, he was a happy little fellow. Liza brought him a bottle of milk. Whilst helping him drink, she noticed the coin lodged in his romper suit.

"What's this, hey baby?" she cooed, her eyes taking in the sight of the demon surrounded in flames upon the old talisman. Petey just giggled and smiled. "Where did you get this?" Liza read the incantation written around the demon. The last word left her lips with a groan at the sound of the doorbell. She rose and left to answer it at once.

Petey clapped his hands on his legs and held his toes with a bemused smile. He could feel the room growing warmer. He watched his biggest teddy glowing orange. From behind it stepped a five-inch tall man with flame-red hair. The granite-like muscular body of the Jinn was clad in yellow and red polka dot shorts and white sunglasses.

"Yes, you summoned me," he began in a bored voice. "What do you— oh no. Baby." The Jinn grew wide-eyed as baby Petey grabbed him with a chubby hand. He began squealing with laughter as he shook the shrieking Jinn like a rattle.

"Waaa! What do you want? Milk, a nappy change, chocolate, teddy bears, dinosaurs, a Ferrari." The Jinn was being shaken all over the playpen. "Ahhh! I'll give you anything, just put – me – daaaaa!" The Jinn was set free and flying through the air. He slammed into a rubber dinosaur, bounced off a squeaking elephant and disappeared in a heap of building blocks.

"Gaaa," said Petey gleefully.

"No, that was not funny." The Jinn dug himself out of the rubble of bricks and faced the baby. "Never do that again," he warned. Petey had other ideas and seized him again. This time the Jinn found himself looking into the wide-open mouth of the baby.

Petey blew a spit bubble as the Jinn grew close to his mouth.

"No way, no sucking and drooling on my hairdo." The Jinn wrestled an arm free and snapped his fingers. "I am not a chew toy. Have a pacifier," he said as the yellow soother appeared, aimed and shot into the baby's mouth. A millisecond later, the Jinn would have become a living gummy bear. Once more he found himself flying across the playpen. This time he vanished and reappeared on one of the pen's posts. A second later a scream filled the air. Liza was back and she was terrified by what she was seeing.

"Why me? I have him throwing me around like a ragdoll and now you screaming at me." The Jinn slapped his forehead. "Can everybody, please, calm down."

"But, but, but you're a, a..."

"Yes woman, I'm a five-inch tall man wearing stylish shorts and sunglasses." The Jinn gave her a disarming smile. "Now seeing as that little monster in there can't read yet, I'll assume you read my coin and summoned me."

"I guess I did." Liza came a little closer. Picking up a toy drumstick, she poked the little man in the chest like he was a diseased rat. "What are you? You won't hurt my baby, will you?"

"Easy lady." The Jinn swatted the stick away. "I'm real, and I'm a Jinn. You summon the big, evil, fiery one if you want your baby fried. You summon me if you want me to do things for you." The Jinn put his palms together. "So, did you need something?"

"Well." Liza took on a thoughtful gaze. "You can change his nappy if you like."

"Ugh, I'd rather throw a lit match in a gas tank than change his stinky nappies. Thank you very much." The Jinn folded his arms. "Next request?"

"Goo, gaa, goo," gurgled baby Petey trying to reach for the Jinn again.

"It's okay, Darling. He's not going to hurt you." Liza moved to comfort her son.

"Actually, he just asked for his daddy to come and have a game with him."

"I wish he could be here, Jinn. Daddy is always at work from seven in the morning until nine at night," Liza told him.

The Jinn whistled. "Wow, that's a lot of hours." The Jinn snapped his fingers. In a moment a car was heard pulling up on the driveway. Liza listened to a person get out and shut the door. Footsteps crossed the gravel, and her husband entered the house.

"Max, why are you home early?" Liza asked never noticing that the Jinn had vanished.

"I was working with a client when I had the strangest urge to come home. I got in the car, and I realised that I really have no time for my darling wife and my special little man." The man took off his suit jacket, picked up his son and pulled his wife into a family hug. "I've decided to significantly reduce my hours. I can still get my work done if I schedule properly. That way, I can also be here for the two of you more often."

"Really? Oh, Petey, isn't that great?" Liza beamed and kissed Max.

"Goo, gaa goo, goo," Petey chuckled and took his daddy's glasses off.

"Really. So, how was your morning?" Max took back his glasses and gave his son one of his dinosaurs instead.

"We had fun in the park, then…" Liza paused and looked for the Jinn. "Came home to watch Petey's favourite TV shows. He'll need a nappy change soon."

"Great well you change his…" Max froze for a second, his eyes glazed. With a shake of his head, he smiled. "I'll change his nappy, then hows about we drive to the seaside for the afternoon," he said instead.

"We'd love that." Liza smiled.

"Okay, won't be too long." Max left the room with baby Petey.

Liza looked about her with furrowed brows. "Hmm, where was the Jinn?"

"He's a model husband now, don't you think?"

said the Jinn. Liza looked into the playpen to see the little man juggling building bricks. He looked every bit the circus clown with those polka dot shorts on.

"He is, thank you so much."

"My pleasure. From now on he will share the chores and be with you both more. Return that love and you will be a happy family." The Jinn vanished and reappeared near the door. "Oh, and don't summon me near that baby again. I have a bloody headache from being used as a rattle!" With that, his job was done. He snapped his fingers and vanished.

The Zookeeper and the Jinn

The City Zoo, a place full of wonderful creatures. A square mile of fun and natural entertainment. Despite that, zookeeper Billy Flanders was not happy. He sighed while walking along the yellow gravel park between the primate exhibits. Walking through throngs of animal ogling people carrying cameras and ice-creams, he looked all about him. A stampede of screaming kids had him diving aside and scowling at their apologetic parents. With a hand on his heart, he shook his head of greying hair and scanned the tree line. He'd lost a young koala and knew he'd be fired if he didn't find it alive. Without warning, a helium tiger balloon on a string struck him squarely in the face. He batted it aside and followed the string to a baby boy giggling in his pushchair.

"Good shot, young man." The zookeeper smiled at him.

"Sorry about that. Petey didn't mean it," said his mother, a woman with a bun of rose-red hair.

"Oh, of course he didn't. Enjoy your day." The zookeeper gave a wave. The lady smiled and walked on never noticing a large coin tinkling to the floor due to a flurry of screaming children.

Billy scooped the silver object into his hand and opened his mouth to call and return it. His eyes took in the horned creature surrounded by flames and his mouth closed again. "This is no ordinary coin."

"Ah, Bill. Can I borrow you?"

The zookeeper looked to see a young blonde lady wearing the zoo's uniform. She was stood waving from an enclosure entrance. He smiled and walked her way. "Hallo, Emily. Haven't seen a koala wandering about, have you?" he asked.

"Sorry, no. I have a swine of a jar I can't open, can you try for me?"

"Sure, let me have it. You should have given it to George. With his strength he'd have it open in a heartbeat." Billy entered the enclosures workroom. He put the coin on the stainless-steel work bench, then took the jar of jam from Emily. "Argh – this is a tough one," he groaned through gritted teeth as he twisted the lid off.

"Yay, well done." Emily grinned having caught the lid as it shot off the jar. "Thanks, for that. What's with the coin, you have there?"

"Not sure it is a coin. I just found it out there." Billy read the incantation encircling the demon on the coin. "What do you think it means?"

"Looks like a talisman from the witchy TV shows, if you ask me." Emily shrugged. Picking up her basket of fruit, she put the jam inside and headed toward the door for the animal living space. "Thanks again, Bill."

"My pleasure, I better go and find this koala," Bill sighed and set off again.

Inside the enclosure, Emily laid out the fruit on the tree trunks and bamboo climbing apparatus. She created pools of jam in log holes to add fun for the animals under her care. Reaching into her basket for more fruit, she furrowed her eyebrows with growing perplexity. The fruit had come from the fridge, yet it was pretty warm to the touch. A creature covered in orange ambled up to her.

Emily smiled at him. "Go on, George. Help yourself."

"Ooh Oo," he said while putting a long arm and hand into the basket. He withdrew a banana and someone else. He raised the banana to his thick lips, and the five-inch tall figure yelled at him.

"No, don't eat me, you, hairy git!"

"Ahhh ahh!" George scratched his backside with his free hand and looked mystified.

"I don't believe it, last time I got used as a rattle by a baby. Now I get summoned to a bloody orangutan."

George the orangutan allowed the Jinn to stand on his open palm and moved his head close to peer at him. The Jinn stood wearing khaki safari shorts and leaf-green sunglasses. His topless torso of red skin was ripped with muscle and as if chiselled from granite.

"What have you got there, George?" Emily moved closer. The Jinn saw her and stretched himself as tall as he could.

"I assume you summoned me. I don't appreciate being forced to deal with manner-less creatures, you know."

Emily just screamed. Several of the orangutans began screeching and bouncing about in a frenzy. George panicked and hurled the Jinn as if he was a bomb. The little man shut his eyes and began praying as he flew out of the enclosure, over a wall and splashed into a small lake.

Surfacing, he gasped for breath while treading water. "One of these days, I might actually get summoned by someone with a little damned respect. I've—"

"These animals are partial to eating children. Please do not lean on or climb over the wall. We feed Goliath, Solomon and Athena enough protein and have noticed that kids give them indigestion." The voice was from a man reading the sign for the enclosure the Jinn was wallowing in. "That's charming," he said before walking away.

The Jinn gulped and drew a deep breath. Something enormous was moving right behind him. He turned to see an enormous gaping mouth, full of menacingly large teeth, dripping with saliva. "Bloody marvellous! Okay, Gator, before you give yourself some Jinn-tergestion, listen up." The little man levitated on to the armoured creature's long snout and stood between his bulbous nostrils. "Here's the deal. You don't eat me, then in return I get you some breath mints – and boy do you need a sack full of those!"

The alligator snapped its jaws loudly.

"That's a no croco-deal then." The Jinn jumped away from the alligator's fearsome maw as the alligator lunged for him. Sensing his summoner, the Jinn vanished in a puff of smoke.

Billy had made it into the avian section of the zoo. He knew a eucalyptus tree grew amid all the cages of squawking and screeching birds. If that pesky koala was going anywhere, hopefully it would there, to feed; after all, koalas eat nothing but eucalyptus. Making a left turn at the owl aviaries, he came into the picnic area. Many families and a school group sat eating among the trees and climbing over the dinosaur playground. Taking out a small pair of binoculars, Billy scanned the branches for his little grey quarry.

"What are you looking for?"

Billy stiffened in fright. The voice hadn't come from anyone close to him – it had come from his right shoulder. He lowered the binoculars and rolled his eyes to the left. He caught sight of the Jinn stood looking at the trees with a smile on his face.

It was too much for the zookeeper. He screwed his eyes tight shut. "Nope, no… There is not a red man on my shoulder!"

"Erm, yes there is."

"No there's not." Billy shoved the binoculars back over his eyes and recommenced his search in the hope that the little man might disappear.

The Jinn took hold of his ear lobe and whispered. "Yes, there is. You summoned me."

"No – I – bloody well – did not." Billy brushed him off and walked to the other side of the eucalyptus.

"Have it your way. However, if you tell me what you're looking for – I might be able to help," said the Jinn opening his arms in a friendly gesture. Billy was aware that nobody else seemed to be noticing the Jinn. Even the family that waved at him as they left the area hadn't noticed him. Feeling he was dreaming, he reached up and poked the little man in the stomach. A gasp left his lips as he felt skin and muscle.

The Jinn scowled. "That's it go on, poke bruises all over me. See if I care."

"Sorry. I... er – I can't believe what I'm seeing and feeling," Billy managed.

"Well, I knew I was handsome, but I don't deserve such a shocked reaction, do I?" The Jinn flexed his biceps and posed for a moment.

"You're a five-inch tall man. That's the shocking bit."

"Well spotted." The Jinn rolled his eyes. "In fact, I'm a Jinn and you summoned me. So, you apparently lost something. How can I help?"

"Yeah." Billy let out a sigh. "I lost a koala. If it gets hurt or remains lost, I'll get fired."

"Ouch!" Well, I'm good with fire. So, I can handle the punishment."

"Yeah that'll help, thanks, Jinn." Billy set off out of the area. At once a person in a hippopotamus suit ran past, scaring some children. It cannoned into Billy, who slammed his shoulder into a cage before he could right himself. The Jinn fell into the cage, landing on a perch inside. He looked up at a large bird with lots of blue and yellow feathers. It turned its black beak and looked at him with a beady eye.

"You're a pretty boy," said the Jinn.

The bird squawked, then swore violently.

The Jinn's jaw fell open as he vanished and returned to Billy looking disgusted. "What sort of zoo is this. Your parrots swear at everybody!"

"Well, that one does, anyway," Billy said, his eyes scanning the trees again.

"I noticed. Oh, look – criminal horses." The Jinn pointed into a paddock, where several equine creatures stood grazing.

"Pardon?"

"They have black and white prison stripes on," the Jinn clarified.

"Those are zebra, and they are supposed to look like that." Now it was Billy's turn to roll his eyes.

"Oh, yeah, my bad. Anyway… lost koala." The Jinn raised a hand and conjured a small flaming arrow. It spun about for a moment before falling still, pointing to a direction forward and left of them. "He's that way."

"Wow, where does a man get a flaming finding

arrow like that?" Billy stood mesmerised by the magic he was seeing.

"When I divorced from my fairy wife, I had to find all my belongings. Rotten woman scattered them over several dimensions, you know. Got this spell from a witch out west. It's kind of neat isn't it?" The Jinn looked proud.

"It's awesome."

"So, koala?"

"Oh, yeah. Come on." Billy started running. The two passed the reptile house. The python with a keeper there made the Jinn glad he wasn't going in that building. The arrow directed them further into the African section. Beyond the elephant and giraffe house, they came to a stop.

"Of course, where else would a koala be," Billy groaned as he picked out the little Australian marsupial high in a beech tree. A tree that just happened to be growing in the middle of a glass-walled enclosure. Prowling – circling below it were three very interested lions.

The Jinn took in the majestic big cats, felt their low rumbling roars in his chest, and grew wide-eyed. "Right, my job's done, then. There's your koala, I'll be going now. Bye." He raised a hand to vanish. Billy caught him about the legs and held him before his face.

"Not so fast, Jinn. I summoned you, right? Now I command you to go in there and rescue that koala."

"Tell you what, I'll magic the lions out here first. Then you can go and get him. How does that sound?" The Jinn looked hopeful.

"*That* is the worst idea I've ever heard. I need to rescue the koala – not have a pride of lions mass-murdering half the zoo's visitors, you idiot!" Billy sighed and walked around to the large barn that was the lion's internal enclosure. "Any chance you can get them in here."

"Of course, I can. You open those hatches and be ready." The Jinn vanished.

Billy entered the building and found the lion's keeper Josh. With a tattoo of a maned lion on his forearm and a matching hairstyle, you might say he loved those big cats.

"Hey, Bill. Not often you come to my neck of the woods, ah?" he said his voice amiable yet deep.

"Hallo, Josh. I lost a koala, and I think your lions are about to eat him. I need to get them in here and rescue him. Can you open the hatches?"

"Oh boy! I can open the hatches. I'm not sure we'll be able to lure the cats in here with a living dinner in the enclosure, though." Josh moved along the caging and pulled some levers throwing the doors for each holding cage open. To his astonishment as each one slid up, a terrified chicken raced in. Behind them came the drooling lions.

Billy watched one pounce on a chicken, go right through it and slam into the cage wall. "Nice one,

Jinn," he breathed as the lion shook off the blow with a quizzical look in its murderous eyes.

"How the hell did you do that?" Josh asked while dropping the hatches again.

"No time. Come on." Billy grinned as he followed the zookeeper into the enclosure. They approached the tree in time to see the koala climbing down with the Jinn riding on its back.

Billy gratefully took the funny little marsupial bear into his arms. "Thanks. Josh," he said before heading back into the zoo a relieved man.

"Well, how'd I do?" asked the Jinn looking smug on the zookeeper's shoulder again.

"Thank you, Jinn. The chickens were genius. You saved this little guy and my backside in one go."

"I'd be lion if I said that was an easy trick to pull." The Jinn gave a cheeky grin.

"You're a real bloody comedian, you know that?" Billy said with a shake of his head.

"I'll be on stage all night." The Jinn floated into the air. "Actually, no I won't. I'll be heading off now. Don't summon me if you decide to get hugged by an anaconda, or lose your pants in the gorilla cage, will you?"

"I won't, thanks Jinn." Billy turned to smile at him, but the little red fellow in the khaki shorts had already returned from whence he came.

The Learner and the Jinn

A midnight-blue Fiesta pulled up at Leon's house. It bore a red 'L' on a white background upon the door panel and bonnet. That simple symbol filled him and many other people with dread. It meant he had to go on his driving lesson. Several sessions in, Leon and the car still did not understand each other. Leaving the house, he walked down the garden path beneath cloudy skies. His face was tense with concern, his legs like jelly. He took a breath and stepped onto the pavement right in front of a cyclist. He slammed on the brakes, hit Leon's shoes, and flew over the handlebars with a metallic crash.

"I… I'm so sorry," Leon managed, having bent to retrieve the bike.

"You blithering twit. Look where you're going!"

"Sorry, I have to take my driving lesson. I'm nervous." Leon noticed the man bore the logo of the City Zoo, with his name Billy Flanders on his green polo shirt. "Are you hurt?"

"Bloody hell, if you drive as well as you walk – we're all in trouble. I better alert the emergency service in advance." Billy rubbed a hand over his greying hair for a moment.

"I said, I'm sorry. You, going to be okay?"

"It's okay. I'm fine," he breathed before getting on his bike and peddling away. Leon shook his head and stepped forward again. It was then something

53

crunched beneath his feet. Stooping, he scooped a large silver coin from the ground. It showed the image of a horned creature engulfed in flames and was like nothing he'd ever seen before.

"Afternoon, Leon. Come on or I'll be late for my next appointment at this rate," called Dave Goodwin, the driving instructor sitting in the passenger seat.

"Hello, sorry." Leon walked around to the driver's seat and slipped inside. As he got comfortable, he looked at the coin in his hand. This time he saw and read the incantation around the mystical looking demon. "Hmm no value, must be a talisman," he mumbled as he put the coin in his pocket and put his seatbelt on.

"You okay?" Dave asked, looking through his black-rimmed glasses at his student. His eyebrows furrowed almost out of sight behind them.

"Yeah, thanks. Just need to calm down a bit." Leon adjusted the seat and mirrors and took a calming breath.

"Okay, start the car when you're ready and proceed. Keep it nice and slow to begin with, please."

"Start when I'm ready..." Leon looked at him. "Can you come back in summer then?"

Dave grinned. "You'll be alright in a minute. Off you go."

Leon started up, made to engage the indicator and swore as the window wipers came on instead.

"Wrong lever." Correcting it, he crunched into first gear and pulled away. The car jerked about as he failed to get the clutch and accelerator working in harmony. Neither student or instructor noticed the increasing warmth and light behind them.

"It's okay, calm yourself a little. We'll go left at the end and drive about a bit to begin with," Dave directed. His attention was taken by groaning and complaining noises coming from behind him. He looked over his shoulder in time to see a five-inch-tall figure with red skin and spiky flame-red hair squeeze out from between the rear seats. The little man thumped onto the cushion and sat up looking rather fed-up.

"Alright, which one of you insensitive gits summoned me into the boot?" he complained while straightening out his police-issue navy shorts, a grey police shirt and aviator sunglasses. He glanced at a star on his shoulder and raised his eyebrows. He'd always wanted to be a police officer. The inch of flab hanging from beneath the shirt would never do though. He snapped his fingers restoring his chiselled abs.

"Waa! What in the world are you?" Dave's voice became squeaky with shock.

"Dave, I'm turning left, what's going on?" Leon indicated and prepared to manoeuvre the car.

"I'm a Jaa!" The car swung to the left throwing the little man off the seat. He slammed into the side window and fell into the door pocket. "Cor, drive slower. This is a car, not a bloody rollercoaster, man," he complained in a muffled voice from the depths.

"Dave?" Leon was struggling to keep his eyes on the road with the events unfolding in the car.

"It's okay. Pull up by the hedge over there and stop," Dave ordered.

"As I was saying. I'm a Jinn. One of you must have summoned me." The Jinn had floated out of the door pocket. Leon saw him and the car lurched forward. The Jinn gulped and shut his eyes. Leon had pulled the car around a parked van, seen the Jinn, panicked, and stomped the accelerator instead of the brake. The car hurtled at the hedge at an alarming speed. Leon panicked as he wrenched at the steering wheel trying to avoid the foliage. The move caused the vehicle to spin out with a screech of tyres and smash through a fence in an explosion of flowers, earth and grass. The Jinn rocketed through the air impacting the windscreen, and Dave swore as he stopped the car on the damaged lawn.

"Phew, I said to stop by the hedge, not mow it down, you idiot!" Dave's knuckles were white from gripping onto the dashboard; his face matched through fearing for his life.

"Have you looked out the window," remarked the Jinn staggering out from a pile of the instructor's paperwork on the dashboard. He took off his broken sunglasses and repaired them with a click of his fingers. "You said park by the hedge, and this car is six-inches from it right now. Next time be more specific as to which side you want it parked on."

"Shut up." Dave glared at the little man.

"The talisman," Leon realised. "I must have summoned you."

The Jinn slapped a hand to his forehead. "I was afraid you might say that. Even I can't make your driving better."

"Sorry, about that. I don't suppose you can fix the garden like you did your glasses, can you?" Leon asked.

"That'd be nice," Dave agreed. He was noticeably forcing his body back in his seat to keep away from the strange fellow.

The Jinn looked out the window and sighed. "That I can do. reverse the car back through the fence you annihilated and get it back on the road – without demolishing anything else if at all possible! Then leave the rest to me."

Leon saw the Jinn vanish in a puff of red smoke. He restarted the car and very slowly reversed back. Nasty crunches and thuds came from the wheels as he crushed everything further on the way out. The Jinn reappeared on the warm bonnet as it stopped on the road. Both instructor and learner watched him go through a series of sparkle-inducing hand gestures. The lawn regrew, the fence mended itself and the flowers reappeared healthier than they were before.

Happy with his work, the Jinn returned to the dashboard looking pleased with himself.

"Did you fix the car?" Dave asked.

"I did." The Jinn looked to Leon. "Don't *bloody well* break it again, will you."

"I didn't mean to." The learner looked at his feet in guilty fashion.

"Thanks to our new friend, no harm done. Proceed down the road; no more than twenty-five miles per hour would be nice," Dave instructed.

"You know," began the Jinn sitting crossed-leg beside the instructor's clipboard on the dash. "I was with another driver once. He said if a car is going slower than him, the driver is a plank. If the car is going faster than him, he is an absolute nutter. What do you reckon, Dave?"

"Just shut up, will you." Leon pulled into the carpark. "We'll try some parking manoeuvres."

"Oh boy. I'll be in the glove box." The Jinn promptly vanished as the car entered the supermarket carpark. Leon followed his instructions and headed for a quieter section.

"Right, draw passed the red car on the right, then reverse back. Apply full-lock to the right and straighten as you park alongside the car. Finish neatly between the lines of your bay if you can."

"Ok." Leon took a deep breath and moved the car into position. "Reverse back, turning on full—" The glove box dropped open with a thud.

"Before you obliterate that car, I have to know something." The Jinn strode out with a black lace G-string hanging from his hand and a big grin on his face. "Dave, is this your spare pair for when learners scare the crap out of you or are you doing after-hours driving lessons of a different kind?"

Dave's face flushed to a colour close to beetroot. "That's my wife's. Put it away, now, please."

"Oh, *really*? Why don't I believe you, hmm?" The Jinn tilted his head and raised his eyebrows in a cynical way, then vanished as the instructor slammed the glovebox flap shut on him.

"Rude, little swine. Erm… do carry on, Leon."

"Okay, and I won't tell your wife." Leon grinned as he began parking the car.

"You can button it an' all," Dave remarked.

Leon just smiled as he completed the parking manoeuvre a few times with reasonable success before driving on again.

The Fiesta was soon heading along a nice straight and empty road. Leon was feeling a little calmer now.

"Okay, this road is perfect. Keep it at thirty miles per hour, then when I give the signal, you must halt the car in a nice smooth emergency stop. Do that by pressing the footbrake and clutch to the floor at the same time while remaining in control," Dave instructed.

"That means, bring the car to a standstill without

hitting everything in sight," put in the Jinn, seated on the dashboard again.

"I'll do my best." Leon gripped the wheel a little tighter; he was nervous again. His eyes moved between the road and speedometer with regularity. He passed houses and trees at a fair speed and then whack. The instructor's hand hit the dashboard. Leon slammed the brake and clutch to the floor. The tyre's screeched and the Jinn shot between the seats. The instructor's clipboard hit him in the face, and the car stopped dead.

"Good job, Leon. Carry on when ready." The instructor sat rubbing his nose as his student restarted the car. He always forgot to grab the board before the car stopped.

"You call that a good job, what was good about that? He turned me into a ballistic missile!" the Jinn grumbled as he freed himself from the rear seatbelt.

"At least he stopped the car without hitting anything," Dave remarked.

"Yeah, I suppose he did." The Jinn returned to the dashboard. "So, from now on, if you hear anyone screaming, see anything hurtling toward you, or Dave covers his head and yells, 'AHHHHH! You idiot you're going to kill someone!', you perform the emergency stop."

"I get the message." Leon followed instruction and made a right turn onto the main road now. Joining the traffic, he negotiated the lights and picked up speed again.

"You did well. Let's head towards your home now." Dave began doing his paperwork as his student drove on.

"I realise you still haven't told me why you summoned me," said the Jinn watching where the car was going. His keen senses told him something was happening ahead.

"Er, I didn't summon you for any reason." Leon could hear sirens now. He was coming up to a roundabout too. "I just read your talisman, and it seems you appeared in the boot. Sorry about that by the way."

"No harm done. Slow down though, something's happening ahead."

"Take the third exit," Dave directed without looking up. The Jinn was no longer sitting. He was standing with his hands on the windshield. Through the long grass on the roundabout, he could just pick out the blue lights of a police car. Leon could hear it but was so focused on the traffic that he hadn't seen it.

"I'd stop for a moment, if I were you," the Jinn advised.

"It's quite clear." Leon pulled into the roundabout, a black van roared round it the wrong way. Then Jinn swore and flinched as the van side-swiped a car with a hollow, crunching bang. It swung onto the verge and fell still. The van was now bearing down on the learner car. Leon yelled, punched the

61

accelerator and spun the steering-wheel hard away. The car shot forward thundering up the curb of the roundabout. There it thumped into the central mound and bounced into the air. The van slewed off the road, slammed into a lamppost and rolled onto its side; a smoking wreck. Dave screamed as the car crashed back to earth in an explosion of soil, debris and flying hubcaps. The Jinn hit the ceiling and fell between the seats.

Leon saw the windscreen crack as his vision filled with long grasses and incoming vehicles on the other side of the roundabout. "I can't steer or stop!" he yelled while wrestling uselessly with the steering wheel.

"Don't panic," said the Jinn in a drunken voice from beneath him.

"Panic, we're going to die you fool," yelled Dave holding on for dear life.

The Jinn rose in front of the shattered windscreen and grew wide-eyed. "Ahh! Oh, no – we're-going-to-CRAASH!"

"Hey, now who's panicking," remarked Leon still trying wrestle back control but getting nowhere.

"I wasn't panicking, I was using screaming as a way to control my emotion." The Jinn waved a hand causing a police car to spin harmlessly out of the way. The learner car regained the road in a hail of blaring horns, and screeching brakes. It hit the back of a sedan, spun back off the road and slammed into a tree with a horrendous engine killing crack. The car stopped so suddenly that the Jinn sailed through the broken windscreen amid a shower of paperwork and disappeared into the foliage.

"Well, we're not dead," said Leon holding his head.

"I am when my boss sees my car." Dave was pale and sounded as if he were in pain.

"Er, yeah. Sorry about that." Leon tried to restart the car. It whirred, coughed some black smoke and burst into flames. "Oh, crap!" he managed with a dumb look on his face. Through the smoke, he saw the Jinn blunder out of the bush.

"There's no time to poop. Get out of the bloody car!" the Jinn ordered, having jumped into the air. He sent sparks flying as he cast a spell. Clouds rolled in, and it began to rain, extinguishing the fire in a cloud of acrid black smoke.

"You saved us, Jinn," Leon said a few moments later. Emergency services vehicles were parked everywhere and the situation was much calmer.

"No, I just stopped you killing us. My advice is: never drive a vehicle again. You're a living health hazard. The road is full of maniacs, and who wants to spend two-thirds of their hard-earned wages on flipping car insurance, anyway?"

"Oh, do you drive where you come from then?" asked Dave.

"No, and after today I'm extremely pleased about that." The Jinn rose into the air. "I'm leaving before you get behind the wheel again. Oh, I hope, I get a nice easy job next time!" he said before vanishing into thin air.

Halloween and the Jinn

"Ah, I *love* Halloween. Nobody ever calls upon a genie at Halloween. Time for a nice long rest and some relaxation." The Jinn snuggled into his hammock slung between two palm trees on the beach outside his home. Despite belief, genies do not live in the talismans and lamps that summon them. The artefact is merely the receptacle for the enchantment that brings forth the demon from Otherworld, a parallel planet, to Earth. Otherworld is split into light and dark sides. The light is home to the good creatures, fairies, kelpie, phoenix, angels, elves and many more. The dark side is home to the worst creatures ever to exist, demons, Cerberus, bogiemen, reapers, vampires and worse. The Jinn used to be of the dark side. Still was if somebody summoned him as that horned fire demon. He hated that form, preferring to be the relaxed shorts and sunglasses-wearing genie he usually was. A friendly brownie had kindly used his magic to ensure only the angriest of humans could summon that irascible ifrit. Since then, the Jinn would only appear in all his sassy bare-chested glory.

"Yoo-hoo! Jinni, darling." That high-pitched voice was like pained brakes being applied on a bus.

The Jinn grimaced. "Yes, Doris, dear."

"Ah, there you are. Comfy, are you?" Doris fluttered over the sand on her dainty swallowtail-like wings. Doris was an overweight tooth fairy with willowy hair, a love of gaudy dresses and a short temper. She was once a wonderful fae in the Jinn's eyes, and he married her to prove it. One-hundred-and-twelve years later they divorced in a bitter moment that led to Doris banishing all his belongings over a dozen dimensions – something he still hadn't forgiven her for. The two had met again a few weeks ago, and thanks to a gnome councillor called Doctor Shulkin they'd begun to rebuild bridges.

"Hmm, this is nice, lying in the sun." The Jinn lifted his sunglasses and grinned.

"Oh, that's good, darling." Doris filled her lungs with air and focused on the Jinn as a gryphon flew overhead. "Now, get your backside indoors and do the laundry!" she bellowed so loudly that the shockwaves sent him spinning out of the hammock with a thud.

"Bloody hell, Doris! I was two feet away not in the other dimension!" The Jinn sat up with his sunglasses askew and sand everywhere. "Doctor Shulkin told you to ask me to do things nicely. Not to yell at me, remember?"

"Yes, I remember. He also said for you to do as I request, often and when asked. I told you ten times to do the laundry. Did you? *Noo!* So, get that cute little red bum of yours in there and do it, *now!*"

"But—"

"Don't but me, Jinni. Go, or I'll curse you into a slimy salamander!"

"Well, at least I'll be a good-looking salamander any—" The Jinn cut himself off as a fiery red glow emanated from his body. It left him grinning like a boy who'd gotten the most Halloween candy.

"Jinni, don't you dare!" Doris made a grab for him, but a human had activated his talisman. The Jinn had been summoned.

"Goodbye, Doris," he said as with a chuckle he vanished into the air.

A genie is powerless to stop a summons. They experience a moment of weightlessness, a bubble of incandescent light that fades as they materialise on Earth. Their talisman is supposed to deposit them before the summoner. The Jinn's coin had never excelled in that respect, preferring to summon him into sticky, painful places anywhere within a mile of his summoner. Today was to be no exception. His senses returned with a shock of loud party music. He was momentarily aware of the dripping-wet, spherical walls that glowed orange around him. He focused on what appeared to be eyes and teeth on one side and gulped. His orange-and-black bat patterned shorts were growing very hot – smoking in fact. He grew wide-eyed and shot into the air. His head hit the roof of the small globular chamber, and he slammed back to the wet floor.

"Ahh! What the hell is this?" he screamed as the whole thing lurched and fell. The tea-light candle he'd appeared on hit him in the face as the object slammed into the floor hard enough to cave it in. The Jinn felt himself rolling end over end a half dozen times before the momentum stopped. He dropped to the floor of the object, covered in juices, singed and dizzy. "Oof, who needs a rollercoaster?"

"Woah! Guys. What made the Jack-o-lantern fall?" asked a male voice breaking through the loud music, somewhere above.

"Ahh, I think it was a ghost. Will you protect me?" replied a female.

"Nah that's not it, boo-tiful. Ghosts don't affect things, poltergeists do that. They throw things, you know," said another voice.

"I reckon, one of you clowns knocked it off," decided the one called Stevie.

"Bite me," replied a vampire girl looking annoyed at the blame being spread in her direction.

The Jinn crawled out of the jack-o-lantern's broken mouth. He was immediately surrounded by a sea of legs in a darkened room. "It fell off because one of you rotten gits summoned me upon the bloody candle in there!" he yelled. Looking up he saw teenagers who looked like walking dead, some grotesquely skewered with knives, others just seemed to be festering with their green skin. He saw a mummified girl, several vampires, a giant bear, witches, superheroes. He opened his mouth to yell again, but a foot slammed into his back sending him flying over the sea of partying people. With no time to react, he smashed through bat and pumpkin bunting and took out a swath of fake spiderweb. Free of that, he let out a cry of fear as he slammed into a wall-mounted skeleton, knocking the legs off. His momentum gone, he plummeted into a bowl causing an explosion of popcorn.

"And pop goes the bloody Jinn," he groaned as he surfaced. "Where's my sum—" He never finished the sentence. He was scooped up with handful of popcorn. He felt himself rise toward an unshaven male face. The Jinn watched the cavernous mouth open. The whole handful of popcorn and the Jinn were going to go straight into that maw of pearly white, minty fresh teeth.

"Don't eat me!" yelled the Jinn unable to free himself.

The boy saw the Jinn in his hand, swore in shock and dropped him. The Jinn fell straight into a Coke glass. It dropped onto its side and rolled off the buffet table. He barely jumped clear as it hit the floor and detonated like a fragmentary grenade.

"What the hell are you doing?" somebody yelled over the music.

"Oh, I hate parties!" The Jinn set off between feet he was forced to dodge in search of his summoner.

"Ahh! What's that, Amy?" Stevie, a vampire,

looked scared of the five-inch-tall, red-skinned man who'd walked past his feet.

"I don't know, but?" the young lady looking like a dead schoolgirl chuckled. "He's so cute. He's wearing Halloween bat shorts and matching bat-wing sunglasses, look."

The Jinn looked down at himself. His talisman always matched his outfit to his summons. He liked the shorts, it was a pity they were tattered and scorched because of the candle. "I'm a Jinn. Which one of you summoned me?" he said as loud as he could to beat the music.

"Aw, he's a cute little Jinn." Amy reached down to touch him and shrieked.

The Jinn opened his mouth and snapped his teeth at her finger like a bulldog. "I'm real. I'm not cute. I'm a muscle-bound Jinn who's not in the mood to be treated like a damned teddy bear. Now, who summoned me?"

"Wow, he's a grumpy little fellow, isn't he?" said a zombie boy with a knife in his stomach.

"Let me set fire to your boxer shorts and see how happy you are then." The Jinn pointed a hand at him.

The boy grabbed his backside. "No, please don't do that. I'm sorry."

The Jinn sighed. "It's alright." He snapped his fingers to fix his clothes and cursed as nothing happened. He tried several more methods without raising so much as a spark. He sighed. "Great, just flipping marvellous!"

"What is it, Jinn?" asked Stevie crouching near him now.

"My bloody magic doesn't work. I…" The Jinn felt a warmth in his chest. He looked about and saw a blonde girl dressed as a princess. The feeling told him she had the talisman. He closed his eyes to teleport to her shoulder. Once more nothing happened, leaving him groaning as he stamped his foot. "Blast!"

"Jinn, you okay? Can we help?" Amy asked.

"I've lost my damned magic." The Jinn folded his arms and took on a thoughtful gaze. "Take me to the princess over there, will you? Keep me low, we don't want the whole room to see me."

"Sure." Amy put out her hand and allowed him to step on to it. "Why do you want her? She's horrible."

"I'm sure she summoned me. I need her help."

"I see." Amy looked at the little man in her hand. "I still think you're cute," she said as she stepped into the crowd.

"Thanks, I guess." The Jinn looked up at his helper and saw her grin. "What?"

"If only you were human size. This party would've been worth coming too."

"Oh, Really?"

"Yeah, there's lots of bedrooms upstairs, you know." Amy gave a coy wink.

"Hell no! I have enough trouble with my partner

Doris without giving her more reasons to yell at me!" The Jinn looked toward the princess. "She's definitely the one. Put me on her shoulder then buzz off and enjoy your evening."

"Aww, that's a shame Jinni, I was just starting to like you," Amy pouted.

"Just do it." The Jinn looked at himself and groaned; he was not representing his kind very well today.

"Hmm, okay. I'll get her away from all these people first." Amy approached the princess and tapped her shoulder. "Harmony, can I borrow you?"

"Ugh, no!" The princess shrugged her off. "I don't talk to people like you at school. Why would I acknowledge you here."

"You snooty sow. Who do you think you are? The ruddy queen?" Amy remembered the Jinn and raised her hand stopping Harmony from replying. "Don't say a word. Just come on."

"Why?" Harmony could see Amy was serious.

Amy took her arm and pulled her outside through a set of double doors made to look like a crypt entrance. The Jinn saw several couples smooching on the patio and amid the darkened foliage of nearby bushes. Amy walked on until she was sure nobody was nearby. She stopped at a small lawned area with a statue and a bench.

"Amy, what's going on?" Harmony freed herself and gave her a stony look.

"Did you read any incantations or spells in the last few minutes?"

"No way, why?"

"This Jinn thinks you did." Amy raised her hand with the little red man standing on it. Harmony sucked in a terrified breath and opened her mouth. Amy lunged with her free hand and gagged her with it. "If you scream, I'll slap you."

"If she screams, I'll slap her too! I've had enough of women screaming at me," the Jinn added. "Harmony, keep your hair on I'm a friend. Now, did you read the words around a fire demon on a large coin?"

Amy removed her hand from the princess's mouth. "Don't scream, just talk to him."

"I… I did." Harmony took the large silver coin adorned with the horned monster and flames from her purse. "My cousin Leon left this on the table. I brought it with me as a fun prop for the party."

"Leon… Oh, yes. The twit who was learning to drive and destroying half the city in the process." The Jinn clapped a hand to his forehead and groaned. Just for once, he wanted to be summoned into a nice calm, relaxed situation.

"Yes, that one." Harmony still looked scared of the Jinn. "W-what are you going to do to me? F-For summoning you, I mean."

The Jinn sighed and shook his head. "I'm not here to do anything to you. I'm supposed to grant you wishes. Trouble is, I have no magic. That means I can't do that, and I can't get home either."

"Aw, you poor thing." Harmony looked a little sad for him.

"I think I know why," Amy said. "It's Halloween. I'll bet the energy it creates to empower witches and ghosts also prevents demons from doing magic."

"That's ridiculous. There's no such thing as witches and demons." Harmony glanced at the Jinn then Amy in a clear state of confusion.

"Erm, do you need to go to the opticians?" asked the Jinn. "If you hadn't noticed – I'm a five-inch-tall, handsome demon!"

"Oh, yeah. Sorry." Harmony had drained of colour. She looked about to faint.

Amy noticed and forced her to sit on the bench. "So, what do we do about it, Jinn?"

"I'm not sure. This has never happened before. Harmony, I can only be summoned by someone who needs something. What were you wishing for when you read my incantation?"

"Erm… A vodka cranberry cocktail…" Harmony had more hopefulness than conviction in her word.

"And, now what were you really wishing for?" The Jinn pressed over the sound of somebody throwing up nearby. "We know she's wishing she didn't have her last drink… And now she's wishing she had a sick bag as well," he added.

"That's gross, Jinn." Amy grinned at him all the same. "Harmony, tell us the truth."

"Oh, alright." Harmony's cheeks flushed a little. "I was wishing my boyfriend would love me as much as his eyes love all the other girls in the room."

"Boyfriend?" The Jinn looked about. "What boyfriend?"

"Exactly. He was supposed to be getting me a drink. Instead, he's off chatting-up all the other girls at the party." Harmony's embarrassment vanished in place of sadness.

"Aw, don't cry over a rotten boy. He's not worth it." Amy made to hug her.

Harmony stepped back. "Thanks, but I'm still not your friend."

"You won't be anyone's friend if you keep playing the snooty princess." The Jinn gave her an unimpressed look. "How do we find this so-called boyfriend without magic?"

"Easy, here's Terry's picture." Harmony offered her phone's screen to the little man.

"Hmm, ugly fellow isn't he? Amy, leave me here with Harmony and find him, will you? Get him out of here by any means necessary."

"Will do, Jinni." Amy put him on the bench beside Harmony and dashed away.

The Jinn turned to Harmony and opened his mouth to speak. A witch stumbled into view, beating him to his tongue.

"Ah, there you is, Harmony. Tha' rotten boy... er boy-boy... er yeah, boyfriend of yours made me a really strong dwink. Now I feel really sick," she slurred, threw-up in the hydrangea and pointed angrily at Harmony or at least where she thought Harmony was anyway. "And it's all your bloody fault.

"Er, Cassidy. I'm over here – that's a statue."

"Oh yeah." Cassidy smiled stupidly. "Hello, Harmony."

"Now, don't you bloody well blame me! You drank what he gave you, so it's your fault."

"I hate you, Harmony." Cassidy lunged forward two steps and staggered three back the other way. "I... I... er— Wow, nice starsies. Oh, yeah. I'll slap you when you stop moving."

"Cassidy, I'm so sorry. Go and find some coffee, okay?" Harmony offered.

"Yeah. Coffee be good. I come back and hit you later." Cassidy scowled and staggered in a circle before her feet pointed her back toward the house.

"And calm down before you head home on your broomstick. You'll only fly off the handle!" added the Jinn catching a funny look from Harmony. "What? Mad witches on broomsticks always lead to witches stuck in trees and broomsticks cracking people over the head."

Harmony laughed at him. "You're hilarious, you know that?"

76

"I try. Doris never appreciates my jokes though."
The Jinn grinned. "Right, here's what I need you to
do."

Amy returned from the Halloween party with Terry
just in front of her. He was walking backwards with
an excited grin on his face.

"So, you single, Amy? I thought you were with
that Stevie. I guess I was too sexy for you to resist,
was I?"

Amy rolled her eyes at him.

Terry smoothed his vampire pompadour. "Yeah,
I was, huh? Are we going to have fun in the bushes?"

"Not a damn chance!" Amy made a frustrated
noise in her throat and scowled at him. It was then
the Jinn jumped from the bush and regained her
shoulder. "Jinni, can I break his nose, please?"

"Maybe in a minute," he said. "Listen up, Terry.
There is a young lady out here who is very upset
with you. You told her you loved her. You don't
do you? No, you're meandering around this party
like a creepy electric eel, trying to see how many
girls you can slither up to, stun and take advantage
of."

Terry scowled. "What young laaah! What the hell
is that, Amy?"

"He's a Jinn." Amy folded her arms across her
chest.

"The lady is Harmony. She gave you her heart,"

the Jinn went on. "Go around this bush to the bench and apologise."

"Oh, I don't know that I owe her one."

"Amy, smack him in the mouth for me, will you?" The Jinn was glad he couldn't do magic; this boy would have never been the same again! He held her ponytail in readiness for a sharp movement.

Amy wound up and stopped short of breaking cartilage.

"Alright, I'm going... Geez!" Terry sighed and continued down the garden.

"What a shame. I wanted to deck him for trying to kiss my friend Becca indoors." Amy followed with the Jinn.

"He'd make a great incubus. What with his talent for lip-locking anything in a skirt." The Jinn made a disgusted noise as Amy came into view of the bench.

Harmony was seated on the bench, surrounded by twinkly pumpkin lights. She had two glasses of wine and slices of cake on a tray.

"Hey, Terry darling. I thought I'd arrange a surprise for you." Harmony tapped the bench beside her with a coy beckoning smile. "Will you come and have a drink with me?"

"Hello, Harm. I..." Terry looked back at Amy. "Sorry... I thought I was going to have some fun out here with her."

"Really, Amy? What is this?"

"He's dreaming. I'd choose never having another kiss, over touching him." Amy raised her hands in surrender, her face twisted with disgust toward Terry.

"Oh, Terry. You, slimy rotten slug!" Harmony stood in her princess dress and stalked toward him.

"Harm, I'm sorry. I—"

Harmony cut him off having swung for him, blasting him in the mouth with a slice of cake. He turned away coughing and spluttering. Amy wound up and slapped him off his feet where he landed with a crack in the rhododendron.

"If we see you hitting on another girl, we'll be sure to tell her what a sorry heart-breaking incubus you are." Amy grinned at the Jinn.

"Now get lost," added the Jinn, while looking worried.

"Thank you, Amy. I should have seen what he was like," Harmony said.

"No worries, we sorted him." Amy raised a hand and gave a little cheer as the girls high-fived.

"We did, come and have a glass of wine with me." Harmony offered the second glass on her tray.

"Thank you." Amy looked to the Jinn. "Seems we changed one person for the better," she whispered.

"We did. I'm still powerless though. I failed to do Harmony's bidding. Now, I don't know if I can ever get home."

"Oh, Jinn you did help me. You showed me Terry was horrible. Now he's gone and I'm happy again. So, thank you."

"My pleasure. I'm glad I helped."

Amy saw a fiery glow emanating from the little man's body. "Jinn, is it?" she asked.

The Jinn snapped his fingers, his shorts and sunglasses vanished, replaced with a white suit. "I'm back baby!"

"Aw, Jinni. I'm so pleased for you."

"Me too!" The Jinn jumped into the air, turned his back and pulled his trousers down, giving the girls a view of his red backside.

"Jinn, that's disgusting!" they said almost together.

"Well, no Halloween is complete without a full moon." He burst into laughter as he flew about the girl's heads.

"I love you, Jinni," Amy said, but she was too late, he'd disappeared in a cloud of red sparkles.

The Jinn reappeared on the beach by his home in Otherworld and right in front of Doris the fairy.

She grabbed him by the scruff. "Gotcha! Get your hide in there and do that bloody laundry, NOW!"

"Hallo, Doris. I was going to. I just came from Dwarf Deli with your favourite rock cakes, look." The Jinn made a paper bag appear in his hand with a single shimmering white rose.

Doris managed a smile. "Aw. Thanks, darling."

"Want to come and help me fold the clothes while I iron, like we used to?"

"Don't push your luck and I might even get us some of our favourite crab apple cider to go with the cakes." Doris led him inside.

"That'd be wonderful. Happy Halloween, Doris."

"Aw, Happy Halloween, Jinni."

Holly and the Jinn

Evening service was due to start within the Workhouse Restaurant. Holly Ward took a breath, tightened her glossy black ponytail and focused on the space around her. A few students from the college were dining at the teak tables by the brown-framed windows. Holly smiled at a group of boys who were chatting about her, among other things. That was nothing new for her, she always just smiled or laughed off the attention. Pausing at the hostess stand, she printed a dinner check. With it on a Workhouse diamond saucer bearing mints, she took it to a couple of girls in the bar corner.

"Here we are. That's twenty-one-pounds-thirty, please."

"Thanks, those Workhouse Burgers are so good," said one of the ladies looking to her blonde friend. "Harmony, are you sure you're okay paying for everything?"

"I told you, it was my treat, Amy. Had you not helped me get rid of that slime ball Terry at Halloween, I'd still be miserable and we wouldn't be friends." Harmony handed Holly some money. "Thanks, that was a delicious meal."

"I'm glad you enjoyed everything. Let me fetch you some change." Holly beamed and swiftly went to the till to cash out the order. Coming back, she found the girls standing and ready to leave. "Here's your change. Thank you for coming, and we hope to see you again soon."

"Thanks, we'll definitely be back soon." Amy smiled. "Right, Harmony lets go and see the film next, shall we?"

Holly set about cleaning the table. "Have a good evening, ladies," she called while polishing the diamond embossed surface. Straightening, her eye caught the light glinting off an object. A large silver coin lay on the seat Amy had been occupying. Holly teased it about in her fingers as she looked for the girls. They were already gone. "Better, put this in the lost property then, I guess," she said to herself. It was then piano music emanated from the stage. Holly gave pianist Tom Bowman a cheery wave and headed for the bar.

"Hello Holly. I'm really sorry I'm late. I got held up in my damned lecture." Waitress Tierney Williams had come out from the back looking immaculate in her chocolate brown Workhouse apron over black blouse and trousers. She looked a little flustered and strained from being late.

"Hello, Tee. It's no problem. Thanks for calling to let me know, though. Everyone's fed and happy in here, so don't worry, okay?" Holly gave her shoulder a squeeze.

"Thanks, Holly. I'll get us ready for service."

"Great, I'm going to fill out a lost property form, then I'm coming back to steal that cute dove hairclip you're wearing." Holly really did think the white bird clip looked stunning in her friend's chestnut ponytailed hair.

"Then I'll be keeping my eye on you." Tierney narrowed her eyes. Both girls were giggling as they parted.

Holly shot into the office for the form and decided to have some tea whilst filling it in. She entered the staff lounge and made herself a cup of Earl Grey. The Ward family ladies rarely drank anything else as was tradition. Sitting at the little round table, she flicked the coin on to the surface with the form. As it settled, she noticed it was etched with a horned demon surrounded with flames.

"So, what are you?" Holly picked out the inscription around the demon. *Evocatus illuc auxilium. Excitandum ditans guttura. Largitor votum meum et vocavi te.*

"Pardon?" said a deep, rich voice.

Holly looked up and smiled at the restaurant's Congolese bartender standing in the doorway. "Hello, Masego. That's Latin. If I remember my granddad's teachings, it means: Summoned to help. Evoked to empower. Wish granter, I summon thee... So, this must be a talisman."

"Be careful then. You might summon a demon." Masego winked and left with a chuckle.

Holly started filling in the form, never realising the kitchenette counter was glowing orange behind her. The splintering crash of a mug slamming into the

84

floor, followed by a volley of swearing caused her to flinch in fright.

"That's it, go on obliterate everything, Jinni! You're supposed to help people when they summon you, not cost them a fortune," came a low female voice.

"Ahh, shut up, Doris," answered a deeper male voice.

Holly jumped off her chair and found her feet surrounded by the remains of a broken mug. She focused on the coffee machine and felt her mouth drop open. There stood a five-inch tall man. He was wearing smart black shorts and sunglasses shaped like a bowtie. The rest of his bare body was fiery red and granite-like with muscles.

"Sorry about the mug. Anyway, you summoned me?"

"I—"

"Of course, she did. Nobody else could have."

The waitress looked for the owner of the shrill voice and discovered an overweight fairy with grey hair. She stood no taller than the red-skinned man. She was wearing a daisy patterned dress and a displeased scowl.

"Doris, darling. I told you, that talisman summons me all over the place. That means, I have to check that I found my summoner to prevent me from granting wishes to the wrong people and getting trapped on Earth." The Jinn sighed and looked up at Holly who was now stood shaking in shock while absently smoothing her ponytail. "Sorry about this. Doris was holding my hand when you summoned me."

"It's – It's okay. I…" Holly thought she was an intelligent girl. Seeing these two little fantastical beings in the staff lounge had her feeling otherwise. Logic told her that either they were real, or she was going insane. "Erm, so the talisman summoned you, right?"

"Yeah, that's it, girl. You summoned my Jinni using that talisman. Now you have to tell him what you want, so we can go home," Doris answered.

"Thank you, Doris. I'm quite capable of doing my job." The Jinn rolled his eyes as he began causing the mug remnants to levitate and glue themselves back together.

"Well, do it then!" The fairy folded her arms and nodded up at the waitress. "I don't know about human men but Jinn's are lazy boars, you know that?"

Holly giggled at the grumpy fairy. "Aw, I bet Jinni does a lot more than you realise."

"Huh, you're supposed to be on my side as a fellow female."

"Sorry, I—"

"It's alright, dear. Jinni makes me mad, that's all. For example, I have to ask him a thousand times to do the laundry."

"But I have six pairs of shorts in the basket to your fifty-two dresses. It's hardly fair." The Jinn set the repaired mug on the counter, then slapped his hips with his hands in frustration.

"Don't you start with the fairness bit, Jinni. I—"

"Hey, that's enough! Both of you hush." Holly gave them both a stern look. "Let's not argue and be friends, please."

"Thank you." The Jinn gave Doris a cheeky smile. "So, have you decided what I can do for you?"

"Yes, you must have wanted something when you summoned him. Or he wouldn't have come," Doris added.

Holly looked at the strange couple on the counter and shook her head. "I don't want anything, thank you."

"There must be something you want." The Jinn glanced up at Holly while scratching his chin. "You're a waitress. How's about help getting a better job?"

"No, I love working here for my mum, and with my team of friends. We're like a happy successful family here."

"Well, that's lovely. How about a hunky boyfriend? Jinni, might be able to help with that." Doris gave a hopeful flutter of her eyebrows.

"Nope, I'm very happy with my darling footballer, Sam, thank you." Holly couldn't help a smile as she thought about him.

"Did I hear my name?" answered a voice edged with huskiness.

Holly felt arms come around and hug her from behind. "Hey, Sam. You did. Are you okay?" she asked as she turned her head to share a kiss with him.

"Hmm. My training went well, thank you, my precious. Who were you talking taah!" Samuel yelped having seen the Jinn and fairy on the counter. "Are they... What are... What's going on?"

"Ooh, he is rather cute and handsome in a sporty way, isn't he?" Doris made kissy lips toward the footballer.

Holly narrowed her eyes at the fairy but never got to retort.

"And I'm not, I suppose?" The Jinn struck a muscular pose.

Doris rolled her eyes at him. "You're so muscly, it's like jumping into bed with a wall."

"I can't believe you just said that. I—"

"Jinn, Doris, stop arguing, please!" Holly groaned, although the feeling of Samuel smoothing her silky ponytail left her relaxed and content. "I think were safe, Sam. I apparently summoned these two by reading that talisman on the table."

"Really? They don't get on well, do they?" Samuel remarked.

"Like two hurricanes fighting over ownership of the Florida Keys." Holly giggled and nestled close to her footballer. "I'm glad we don't have that problem."

"Me too, I love how we can talk about things." Samuel looked to the Jinn. "You should adopt that philosophy, both of you."

"We've been trying, believe me." The Jinn grinned and snapped his fingers. "She doesn't wish for anything. Do you want something?"

Samuel made a musing noise. "I know – the flower shop was shut. Can you magic Holly some flowers for me?"

"Sure, which kind? Marigolds…" the Jinn made an orange bloom appear before him.

"Yeah, there's a pair of those under the sink. You can do the dishes with them, when we get home," Doris ordered.

"Whatever, darling." The Jinn pulled a face and sighed. "Where were we… ah, maybe you'd like some chrysanthemums, peonies or sunflowers." The Jinn made each appear as he named it. "Perhaps some anemones, daisies or caedes flowers – ow!"

Doris had slapped him for conjuring the vicious toothy-looking black flower. "Idiot! He wants to profess his love to Holly, not have her eaten by a carnivorous plant!"

Holly saw the fearsome plant lick its petals before the Jinn vanished it.

"Sorry! I was having a little fun with that one," he said. "What about these?" The Jinn waved his hands and made some stunning Asiatic lilies.

89

Holly sneezed violently. Less than a second later she sneezed again.

"Jinn, get them gone quick!" Samuel demanded having grabbed some kitchen roll for her.

"Whoops, allergies. My apologies." The Jinn vanished the lilies with a guilty look at Holly who looked most uncomfortable just then.

"It's okay, you didn't know about my silly nose," Holly said nasally as she took the tissue and blew her nose.

"I'm still sorry. Right, Sam. Try these." The Jinn conjured a bouquet of beautiful red and pink roses.

"Those are perfect." Samuel took them out of the air. "A magical bouquet for the enchanted lady who holds my heart."

"Aw, thank you, sweetheart." Holly accepted them and brushed her nose against his as they shared a kiss.

"Ahh, so romantic." Doris knitted her fingers before her. Looking to the Jinn her enamoured look vanished. "Why don't I get roses like that, huh?"

The Jinn created a matching smaller bouquet. "There you go darling."

"Aw, thank you, Jinni." The fairy dived on and assaulted him with kisses.

"Bloody hell, woman. I knew there was a reason why I didn't get you flowers." The Jinn shook free and smiled at her. "You are welcome though."

"That's much better you two." Holly smiled at them.

"Thanks." The Jinn looked at himself. He wasn't glowing. "You have to wish for something or I can't go home."

"I can't." Holly moved to put her roses in a vase. "I don't want anything. What do you wish for Jinn?"

The Jinn sucked in a breath and blinked at her. "Who me? Nobody, ever asked me that before. Hmm…" The Jinn glanced at Doris who was looking expectant, then at Holly who nodded, urging him to say something. "I'd like a week with no summonses that I can spend in Fairy Wonderland with my darling Doris."

"Aww, that's sweet." Holly beamed.

"Would you really do that?" Doris gave the Jinn an interrogating look.

"If I could, yes." The Jinn put an arm around her. "Seriously, Holly, I need a wish from you."

"Okay, I wish for an apple custard danish pastry for Sam. Some millionaire's shortbread, for me…" Holly put her roses on the table and hugged Samuel again. "And a free week in Fairy Wonderland for you."

"Fantastic! Consider it done." The Jinn took Doris by the hand and snapped his fingers. "Thanks for the freedom, goodbye my friends," he said as he and Doris glowed red and vanished in a cloud of glitter. A pair of thuds on the table caught Holly's attention. There waiting for her were two huge plates; one loaded with danish pastries, the other stacked with millionaire's shortbread.

"Hmm, snack time," she said.

"I think my football trainer is about to get annoyed with me." Samuel gave Holly's ribs a tickle making her squeal, then danced away from her. He picked up a danish and bit into it. "Hmm, thanks for wishing for these."

"My pleasure, sweetheart." Holly tried a shortbread. "Wow, these are delicious."

That evening Holly was driving her and Samuel home in her sky-blue and black trimmed Mini Cooper. She pulled over by the park.

"Why are we stopping?" Samuel asked.

"I have to pass this talisman on. I realise that the girl didn't lose it. Magic coins like this never stay with one owner." Holly climbed from the car and entered the dark park beneath the velvety starscape, holding her footballer's hand.

"Shouldn't you try to keep it. I mean to be able to summon a Jinn and make wishes is a great tool, isn't it?" Samuel looked at Holly in her Workhouse uniform. He'd fallen in love with her wearing that in this very park a couple of years ago.

"It sure is." Holly led him to the wishing fountain in the centre of the park. She glanced at all the pennies reflected in the lights beneath the shimmery water and smiled. "Yes, this is where is needs to go."

"You sure? What if you need more millionaire's shortbread and danish though? What if you need the Jinn for something else?"

"I don't need the Jinn, Sam. I have my family, my friends, a lovely restaurant and most of all you, sweetheart." Holly turned her back, closed her eyes and flipped the coin over her shoulder. It splashed into the water behind her. "I don't wish for or need anything else to be happy," she added while watching the coin sink through the rippling water of the fountain.

"Hmm, so long as I have you I'll always be happy too." Samuel wrapped her in his arms. "You did wish for something before throwing the coin though, didn't you?"

"I did. I wished for the coin to find its way to somebody who really deserves and needs it." Holly felt truly content as she returned to her car and drove them home that evening. As for the talisman, we'll soon see where it ends up next. You will join the Jinn to find out, won't you?

The Homeless Man and the Jinn

Rupert Hutton was homeless. He'd been a wealthy businessman until a couple of years ago. Now instead of a nice comfortable home, he lived in a doorway with a single duffle bag of possessions. He was no victim of recession or joblessness; his fate had been much worse. He could handle wearing his stinking, scruffy suit. Even his long unkempt hair and itchy beard weren't completely unbearable. No for Rupert it was cold, harsh rain which left him miserable about his situation.

This evening like most, Rupert had gone to the park. It was drizzling but a few stars were beginning to peak through the clouds. Rupert liked to walk among the borders and enjoy the lights of the city twinkling around him. It was especially nice after dark as nobody else would be there. Mr fox was about rummaging in the bins for food. Rupert smiled at him and perched on the marble side of the wishing fountain. He loved the gentle light shimmering from the fittings beneath the water – creating a soft relaxing glow. He'd often sit here and reminisce over the life he once had. Rupert had a secondary purpose for his visit. Checking the coast was clear, he slipped a hand into the water and scooped a handful of coins from the bottom. Many people came and tossed a coin into the fountain to make a wish. Rupert was well aware the coins were collected by the city council and used to make the councillors ever richer. Knowing this, taking a few to buy coffee wasn't so wrong, was it?

Leaving the park, he crossed the road to his home. He always stayed in the Top-Boy Fashions doorway of a night. It was deep and had a good roof covering against the elements. Reaching the recess, he let out an anguished groan and shook his shaggy head. The space wasn't his anymore; a young man and his girl were hunkered in a sleeping bag inside now.

"Please, leave us. We have nothing but each other," said the drawn, sad-looking man. He reached into the sleeping bag and drew a large flick knife. "Please, just go away!"

"Okay, take it easy! I know the feeling of having nothing, friend." Rupert raised his hands and took a calming breath. "Look, you can have my doorway. I just want my bag, that okay?"

"Y-yeah sure, okay." The man put himself before the girl and watched suspiciously.

"Thank you." Rupert reached into the doorway and retrieved his duffle bag from a dark corner. The old army-issue bag was filthy and had a tear where the zip was coming away. It still did the job and would continue to do so for now. "Good luck, friend." Rupert left as quickly as he could.

Rupert could have cried over losing his doorway. He felt homeless all over again, as he walked along the dark, cold street. Taking an alleyway, he came up behind some shops and sank against the wall between large rolltop bins and a pile of black bags.

"Damn you! Why can't you just let me have the little I have and leave me be!" he let out a sob and wiped away the tears which flowed into his scruffy beard. Digging into his suit jacket pocket, he found just one large coin. Looking into the pocket, he realised a new hole had robbed him of the rest of the change he'd collected from the fountain. Placing his shaking hands over his face, he sat back against the wall in silent, wretched tears. He didn't know how long he sat there disconsolate and heartbroken. It was only as his melancholy abated, he remembered the large coin. Holding it in his dirty hand, he saw it was no currency at all. It bore the image of a demon surrounded in flames. He bit on it. *It's solid metal,* he thought. *Maybe I can sell it for a little real money.* Peering closer he saw and read the inscription around the demon. *Funny thing. I'll wait until morning and try and sell it*, he decided having laid back against the wall and closed his eyes in the attempt to sleep.

Something thudded among the black bags – a rat most likely. The rubbish began to glow orange, exuding heat as something smashed within the bags. Rupert snapped upright in time to see a bag catch fire as a little red-skinned and muscular man dived from it, rolling under the bins.

"Marvellous! Thank you very-bloody-much for summoning me into a pile of rubbish!" he said in a strangely deep voice for his five inches of height. He stalked out from beneath a bin and snapped his fingers, extinguishing the burning rubbish. Disaster averted, he folded his arms and glared at Rupert.

"I... er my apologies." Rupert blinked, rubbed his eyes and shook his head – he couldn't believe what he was seeing. The little man had torn denim shorts and a woolly, blue Beanie hat on his head. "Wha— err. What are you?"

"I'm a Jinn, and I'm having a bad day. First Doris throws a bucket of vegetable peelings at me this morning and now you summoned me into the bleeding trash!" The Jinn took a breath and wrinkled his nose. "*Phew*! You haven't had a bath in a while. Are you a vagrant?"

"Homeless."

"Same thing. Well, you summoned me. I guess you'll be wishing for money, a house on the beach and a holiday in Vegas, right?"

"I actually had all that once." Rupert's eyes welled with misery again.

"Really?" The Jinn summoned a little armchair and some popcorn. Both appeared with a click of his fingers and a flash of red glitter. He sat down and wriggled into a comfortable position. "Okay. So, what happened?"

"I was a well-paid insurance company manager. I had who I thought was a lovely wife in Gerri and a son and daughter. I was so proud of those kids."

Rupert fell silent; tears left track marks through the dirt on his cheeks. He rummaged in his bag, took out a photo of his family and looked at them with a sigh.

"Here, have some tissues." The Jinn made a pack appear in mind air. He watched Rupert take them and dry his eyes. "Sounds like you had it good. How'd it go so wrong?"

"Thanks. I... Erm. I had to be away from home a lot to work – that was the trouble. I'd leave Monday morning and return Friday night most weeks. One Friday two years ago, I got home to discover a nightmare waiting for me. My home wasn't mine anymore. Gerri had waited for me to leave on the Monday. She packed our family out of the house, sold it and all my belongings leaving me with nothing."

"What! *Wow* and I thought Doris was a pain in my backside pheeew!" The Jinn whistled in shock. "I mean that just plain nasty."

"I know, right? I stayed in my car that weekend. Monday, I went to work and I'm summoned to the general manager's office. Gerri has reported me to the police accusing me of assaulting her. Damn it, Jinn. I would never touch a hair on that woman's head. I loved her and my kids so much..." Rupert paused to take a breath and stop himself shaking with anguish. "My company couldn't have anyone on any form of charges working for them and so my manager fired me on the spot."

"Despicable!" The Jinn sat opened mouth on his

armchair. His popcorn spilt and forgotten around his feet through his growing anger at Rupert's predicament.

"I tried to fight, but Gerri had found a new man and screwed me over rotten. I fought everything but lost. While I was acquitted of the assault, I ended up homeless, jobless and worthless in days. I've been like this ever since."

"I'm so sorry you suffered so much. You know, the only thing worse than your situation is having to travel through countless dimensions looking for your boxer shorts." The Jinn stood and started pacing. "So, how much do you want to get out of this situation?"

"About as much as you really wanted to find your underpants apparently," Rupert managed a small grin.

"Those boxers were the most comfortable pair I ever had. And... Why the hell are we discussing my boxers?" The Jinn glared at the homeless man.

"You started it." Rupert pointed a dirty finger then sighed. "Anyway, I can't get out of this. I can't have a job without a home and a rubbish-strewn alley doesn't count. I don't want to wish for piles of money either. I don't deserve that."

"Good, I can't conjure you any money anyway." The Jinn vanished his chair and stood tall. "Are you any good with mobile phones?"

"New-fangled contraptions," Rupert mumbled. "I hate them."

"Oh good – that makes two of us." The Jinn grinned. "Time to learn all about the curse of mobile devices."

The following morning Rupert did the best he could to tidy himself up. He took up a newly made sign that read *'Make a donation and I'll solve all your mobile device problems'* and headed for the high-street. He sat in a good position not far from a mobile phone shop and started plying his new trade. To his delight, he was soon unlocking contracted phones, teaching tips and tricks, removing tracing software, installing apps, and fixing broken phones for many people.

"There we are, sir. Now your phone will install any app from any platform you desire," Rupert said to one man wearing a suit and carrying a briefcase.

"Thanks." He took back his phone and turned to leave.

"Excuse me. You didn't make a donation." Rupert pointed to his sign and the bucket he was collecting in.

"Tough luck, beggar." The man smirked and made to walk away. It was then his briefcase flopped open spilling paperwork everywhere.

Rupert scooped up and returned some of the papers. "Rough justice, friend. You were greedy and you paid for it in seconds," he commented.

"Think yer funny do yer?" The man stuffed his

papers in his bag, turned to leave, and his belt broke, allowing his trousers to slip right down to his shoes.

A lady screamed having gotten an eyeful of his boxer shorts. "You dirty man!" She belted him with her handbag and dashed away.

"Ouch! That Karma really is kicking your arse today, isn't it?" Rupert stifled a grin and looked up at the Jinn sitting on the very top of a lamppost.

"What are you up to, beggar?" The man turned on him.

"Me? Nothing. Oh, and I'm not begging. I'm offering a service and excepting donations for it." Rupert listened to a young man then took his phone. He tapped away on it for a few moments, making it work again. The owner paid him five pounds for it and left as a car pulled up to the curb.

"Smart arse!" The man bent to restore his trousers. He turned to leave again, and wham! the car door flew open, knocking him on his backside.

"Damn! You are having a bad day!" Rupert grinned as he took and fixed a tablet for another few pounds.

"I don't know what this is, pal, but I'm getting mad!" The man took out his wallet and threw a ten-pound note into the bucket. This time the Jinn let him leave with a big grin on his face.

When night fell, Rupert had amassed quite a sum of money. He counted it with a smile on his face. "I want to thank you, Jinn. This is amazing, and it was so rewarding earning it myself."

"It was equally as much fun ensuring you got paid." The Jinn was sitting on his shoulder now. "You did good, but we're not done yet either."

"Oh really! What's next?"

"That depends on how much you want to grow and be successful from here."

"So long as I can work for it and earn it – I'm willing to do anything to get it." Rupert beamed at his pile of money. "I still can't believe this."

"Well, you should. All I did was impart some knowledge and you did the rest." The Jinn created a shower of sparks with a snap of his fingers. "I didn't even use any magic."

Rupert went back to work on the high-street fixing technology for the rest of the week. By the weekend he'd amassed enough to rent a little room and buy a new suit. With a haircut and shave, he looked like his old self. The Jinn taught him more every day and pointed him in the right direction. By the end of the month, he'd gotten himself a job in at Gadgi-Tech computer and phone store as a technician. He surpassed his role in a week and soon had the manager's position. It was then it happened.

Rupert was reprogramming a tablet while talking to its owner. The Jinn was sitting on a shelf of laptops, tablets and phones which Rupert had gotten ready for customers to collect. He'd made himself invisible to everybody except Rupert and was enjoying watching customers browsing the aisles of technology.

"There we are, sir. Now it works as intended." Rupert gave him a smile and sent him on his way. Rupert was a new man in his suit and tie and well-groomed hair. He looked up swore under his breath and looked to the Jinn. "On no, Jinn you have to help me. That's Gerri, she'll ruin everything!"

"Relax. Be nice so she can't get you fired and it'll be fine." The Jinn rubbed his hands together and lay in wait.

Rupert took out a laptop and read the repair order label on the case.

Gerri dressed in a simple black skirt, a cream t-shirt and a regular coat browsed a while.

Rupert couldn't help following her with his eyes until she spotted him and came over. To Rupert's shock, she had tears in her eyes as she arrived at the counter.

"Hey, Ruppy. I didn't expect to see you again. I heard you were living on the streets. I'm really glad you're not," she said.

Rupert locked his eyes on the laptop, reading the blue screen that appeared. He hated the fake affection in her voice. "Gerri. Can I help you?"

"Oh, Ruppy. I made a terrible mistake two years ago." Gerri leaned on the counter provocatively.

"You want that USB cord?" Rupert bit his tongue while trying to diagnose the boot issue on the laptop.

"No, I want a second chance."

Rupert was seething. He took a deep breath forcing himself not to rise. "I'm working. Are you buying that cord or not?"

"Look, I met a man who made me and the kids feel so loved. He made me sell our home and live with him. I—"

"I don't care, Gerri. Slither back to him if you like." On the desk, the laptop began rebooting itself without a hitch.

"I can't. He kicked me out for a younger model. Me and the kids live in a two-bedroom flat now. You can visit them if you like." Gerri delved into her handbag and produced her phone. "What's your number? I'll text the—" Red smoke started issuing from her phone.

"What about the restraining order?" Rupert turned his back and smiled at the Jinn.

"Oh, don't worry, Ruppy. I'll have it lifted for you." Gerri swore at her phone. "Can you fix this?"

"No, it's fried." Rupert hid a smirk.

"Shame. Please, Ruppy. Me and the kids really need you." Gerri scratched her nose.

Rupert watched her scratching it for a long few moments. "Got an itch?" he asked as she scratched again.

"Yeah, a really bad one." Gerri continued to rub at her reddening nose.

"Perhaps you shouldn't lie then." Rupert put the repaired laptop away. "You're not ruining my life twice. However, if you agree to lift the restraining order, I'd love to spend time with the kids again. Maybe I could have them come to my place once in a while too. Beyond that, goodbye, Gerri." Rupert decided to leave his desk and get away from her.

"But, Ruppy. I still love you and we can get back together." Gerri put her hand on his shoulder as he came around the counter.

"No, you love money. Goodbye." Rupert shrugged her off and walked into the first aisle.

"But I love you, Rupargh!"

Rupert spun on the spot in time to see smoke erupt from Gerri's skirt. She leapt about a foot in the air, screamed and fled the shop at top speed. "Jinn, what did you do?" Rupert asked with a little glee about him.

"She was a dirty rotten liar. So, I set her pants on fire." The Jinn said it without emotion but couldn't stop his face lighting up with a big grin. He hadn't done that in a while.

"Thanks, Jinn. Shame she left without paying for that USB cord." Rupert burst out laughing as he headed for the canteen.

"Well, she's dealt with. You have a new, happy life. My work here is done." The Jinn looked pleased with himself walking along the tops of computer screens on the shelf.

"I want to thank you for your help. You allowed me to get a decent life back. To get my confidence and smile back. I'm eternally grateful to you for that," Rupert said.

"Don't be, you did it. I just gave you some information and an idea. You did the hard work while I had a little fun. Remember this to everyone you meet, anyone can do anything if they just work hard enough to achieve it." The Jinn levitated into the air. "It's been fun, Rupert."

"It has, good—" Rupert smiled. The Jinn had vanished in a shower of red glitter. Shaking his head with a grin, Rupert left for a sandwich. He was going to keep working, he had his eyes on the general manager's chair now.

The Ethical Hacker and the Jinn

"Gadgi-Tech." Kelvin read the computer store sign above the entrance and stomped inside out of the rain. He paused to wipe his glasses off with a grumble. "I may as well live in this piggin' place!" Ignoring the phone and television departments, he went straight for the computer section. He selected USB leads, a pack of microfilters and a large memory stick. Approaching the help desk, he caught the eye of the server and technician Rupert Hutton. Kelvin knew he hadn't been on staff long, but he was very good at his job and the two had become friends. It was hard to believe Rupert in his smart suit used to be a homeless man living in a doorway by the park. Kelvin admired him for how he'd changed his life around.

"Hallo, Kelvin. It's not all good news, I'm afraid." Rupert took a box from the customer collection shelf and came to the counter.

"I thought as much. What's the verdict? Have I lost everything?" Kelvin rubbed his face stressfully. Sometimes he hated computers with a passion.

"The patient is as dead as a technically advanced dodo. However, the phoenix rises from the fiery microchips – you see, I was able to get your data from your hard drive and implant it into this new one for you." Rupert patted the box with a victorious grin.

"Oh, you star! You just saved my life." Kelvin wrung his hands and smiled for the first time in days.

"My pleasure. I found something weird when I took your old hard drive apart."

"Really? What?" Kelvin dreaded the coming answer.

"Well, the ribbon cable inside was twisted into a nice neat bowtie. I've never seen anything quite like it."

"That is weird... Anyway, thanks again, Rupert. What do I owe you for the hard drive surgery and these?" Kelvin put his purchases on the counter and took out his circuit board design wallet.

Rupert rang the purchases into the till and bagged everything. "That's eighty-nine, ninety-five, please."

"And worth a fortune in recovered data too." Kelvin paid in notes, never realising he received an unusually large and abnormal coin in his change. "Thanks, man."

"See you next week." Rupert gave a cheeky salute.

Kelvin rolled his eyes, waved and left for home. He wanted to get back and check his data really was okay – as soon as possible.

Kelvin lived in an apartment within view of the river. It wasn't big or beautiful, but it suited his needs. The little white kitchen had a microwave to nuke a reasonable meal when he forgot to order pizza. The bedroom was a place to crash; it didn't need to do anything else. The lounge was the furthest from a resting space as you could get. A sweeping desk of monitors, keyboards, modems, game controllers, circuit boards, pen-drives with yellow ducks on them and an assortment of fast food cups and boxes filled one wall. To its right, a tv screen was mounted on the wall. It was playing a space show on a sci-fi channel as Kelvin came in with his bag in one hand and a pizza box in the other. His eyes ran over his collection of comic book character figurines as he dumped his bag on the cluttered sofa. He loved superheroes above even technology. He threw off his Krypton trench coat and collapsed into his big leather swivel chair with a sigh of relief. Going out was always an anxiety-inducing experience. Still being able to sit and devour a five-cheese, three-pepperoni, sweet-pepper, bacon, barbecue pizza, hold the pickles, was well worth it.

With his pizza devoured, he threw the box on the pile burying the sofa, chucked his wallet on the desk dislodging some coins and unpacked his new hard drive. As the computer booted, he noticed his low WIFI speed with a disdainful scowl. Pulling out the new microfilters, he ducked beneath the desk to install them in the phone socket. They were his last hope to boost his speeds. Crawling out, his hand brushed the tower of plugs. The spaghetti junction of electrical cable shocked him. He flinched backwards, bashed his shoulder on the desk, dislodged his glasses and scattered disposable coffee cups and gadgets on the floor. Amid them, something hit him over the head. "Aww, blast my luck!" he cursed while searching for his glasses.

Finding his spectacles amid the debris, he shoved them back on his nose. Looking through the lenses again, he felt his focus returning and noticed the odd coin sitting on the floor.

"That's weird," he muttered as he picked up the talisman with a hand over his sore shoulder. He took in the horned demon surrounded with flames and read the inscription around it. "Rupert must have paid me with you." Kelvin hurled things back on the desk and sat down again never realising an old computer tower had taken on a red glow. He tapped away on his keyboard, never noticing smoke issuing from the CD Drive. "Bloody great, HHD Error – Oh wait; new hard drive. I have to let it install its driver's fir—" Bang!

Kelvin almost fell off his chair as the computer tower erupted in a flash of fire. The sides fell off and the CD drive shot out. It rocketed across the room like a cruise missile, decapitating several superheroes on the shelf. Kelvin's mouth fell open and his glasses almost fell off his face as he watched on in shock. A five-inch tall figure emerged from the smoky interior of the computer tower holding a circuit board. As though chiselled from rock, the red-skinned demon blinked and looked about through thick, black-rimmed glasses. He had on large red boxer shorts, bearing images of computer mice and a slogan, *If you like my mouse, check out my stylus baby!*

The Jinn peered about as if struggling to see. Eventually, he spotted his summoner and scowled. "Thanks a bunch! That was my most painful summons in a while." He held up the circuit board. "I don't know what this is, but it brained me in there."

"Figures, it's a... Erm – it's a memory card." Kelvin gulped as he cleaned his glasses and tried to figure out whether to believe his eyes or not. "What are you?"

"I'm a Jinn. You summoned me." The Jinn squinted about him and took the geeky glasses off. He smiled as his vision cleared. With a snap of his fingers, he turned the glasses into designer shades before putting them back on. "That's better. I hope you didn't summon me to clean this room out – it looks and smells awful in here!"

"Sorry about that, I have a lot of work to do. I work with big companies to detect holes in their security as an Ethical hacker you see." Kelvin opened his arms and shrugged apologetically.

"Ethical hacker? Last time I saw someone get hacked it was on the football field – there was nothing ethical about that let me tell you!" The Jinn walked through some of the gadgets, turning his head to look at them. "What all this stuff?"

"Well, that's a WIFI pineapple." Kelvin pointed to a gadget with lots of antennae. "That allows me to find, use and penetrate any device or security network so long as I have a WIFI signal I can use."

"Hmm, sounds painful." The Jinn scratched his head. "What's this?" He indicated a green circuit board with lots of ports and components attached.

"That's a raspberry. It—"

"Ha! Like to see you try and eat that with your fruit salad!" The Jinn gave it a kick. "You wouldn't need a Jinn then, you'd need a good dentist!"

"I didn't name it." Kelvin grinned. He liked this sarcastic little guy. "I just use it like a hacker's Swiss Army Knife. It's like a mini-computer that allows me to manipulate so many things when trying to execute entry into computer portals and servers."

"Ahh, now, portals, I know about. Don't try and enter one of those unless you know what you're doing. Trust me, it's no fun getting your anatomy rearranged. I once knew a brownie who made that mistake; he walked around with his head stuck to his arse for a fortnight until I managed to repair the damage."

"Wow! Poor guy," Kelvin said.

"Yeah, he reckoned taking a crap was a nightmare. At least he could see what he was doing with his toilet paper though." The Jinn roared with laughter and ended up holding his sides.

Kelvin chuckled too. "Oh, I see, you're a big

joker," he remarked while tapping away on his keyboard.

"I do like to have a little—"

Kelvin slammed his hand down on his keyboard furiously. "What do you mean internet connection lost? Stupid damned computer!" he blustered at the screen.

"Wooo! That inanimate object really knows how to make you mad, huh?" The Jinn folded his arms and grinned up at him.

"Shut up!" Kelvin retorted, now stabbing his keyboard with furious fingers as he attempted to diagnose the problem.

"Fine." The Jinn vanished in a puff of smoke and reappeared on the shelf of superheroes. "If you tell me what's wrong, I might be able to help," he volunteered, having taken hold of a Superman figurine by the shoulders. He gave it a shake and a slap to see if it was alive.

"Agh! No – put that down now! You already killed two of my prized figures." Kelvin indicated the decapitated heroes on the floor with the smoking CD Drive. That one is a limited edition and worth a fortune."

"He's a bit crude, having his underpants on the wrong side of his trousers, isn't he?"

"Says you walking about in your boxer shorts," retorted Kelvin, resorting to swearing at his computer again.

The Jinn returned to the desk and put on a swagger. "I do, but at least I make these look good. Don't you…" The little man flashed out of existence as Kelvin punched the desk, sending coffee cups flying across the surface. "…Geez! Calm down before you break your hand!" he said having reappeared sitting on top of the screen.

"Sorry. This thing drives me mad. It must have gremlins or something." Kelvin slumped in his chair and sighed.

"Did you say – gremlins?" The Jinn dropped down on the keyboard and began hopping about the keys.

"Yeah, it's gotta be by the number of times this heap of neurons has gone wrong."

"Yeah, I'm not surprised. The *Gremian Vexii* – or 'little pain in the arse' commonly known as a gremlin – has a knack of making any sort of machinery malfunction. They began slipping into your world when the aviators learned to fly. They…"

"Wait, Jinn. Are you saying gremlins are real?" Kelvin sat up and looked at him in shock.

"Oh, yeah. They're real alright. Let's see if you have one." The Jinn stood in front of the computer screen and rolled up his imaginary sleeves. Raising his hand, he said, *"Gremian aperio,"* and shot a bolt of indigo light at the screen.

"Wah!" Kelvin recoiled in fright. "Don't blow up my computer! I… still… need…" he spluttered to silence, his eyes widening as the screen grew bright and millions of windows, webpages, executables and documents began opening, closing and flashing all over the screen. At the same time, all manner of horns, bells and whistles began blaring from the speakers.

"Yup – you got a gremlin!" The Jinn hit the screen with another blast of indigo magic. This time a blue fog grew out of the screen. It ejected a skinny, sallow-looking grey figure wearing denim overalls and a lurid red shirt. He shrieked as he landed on his head, rolled a few times and slammed into the mouse.

Standing, he staggered about until he shook off a cross-eyed look. He revealed himself to be an inch taller than the Jinn (not including the last few strands of his wispy grey hair) and just as rude as he promptly flipped his middle finger at him. "That bloody 'urt!" he complained while rubbing his pointed nose.

"Huh, Marlin. What are doing here? I see your manners haven't improved."

"'Allo, Jinn, 'ow the devil is ya? Doris alright, is she?" Marlin beamed making his thin lips and dark eyes appear like those of a friendly gargoyle. He came over, ears flapping as he clapped him on the back.

"Hi, Marlin. Doris is fine thanks."

"Jolly good! You should see that guy up there when I cut 'is internet connection or make 'im think 'e's 'itting all the wrong keys – Woowee! 'e gets boiling mad, 'e does."

"I noticed," said the Jinn leaning against the printer looking unimpressed.

"Excuse me. Are you saying you caused all my computer problems?" said Kelvin leaning in close with fury narrowed eyes.

"Oh, yeah, matey. Bin 'aving a lot of fun for the last few weeks, I 'ave." Marlin grinned. "Thank ya very much for the entertainment."

"Entertainment!" A vein began pulsing in Kelvin's forehead. "I should bloody kill you for all that hassle you caused and for ruining my hard drive, you little b—"

"Kelvin! Calm down you'll blow a fuse. I'll…"

"Ooh! Don't you worry about that. I've got a collection of fuses. Big ones, little ones, 'eavy duty ones. You tell me what amperage you is needing and I'll fetch it for you," Marlin said looking pleased that he might be able to help.

The Jinn slapped his forehead. "I don't even want to know where you're getting those from."

"Well, you see," Marlin put his hand over his mouth and carried on in secretive tones, "these 'ere 'umans is needing them to protect and earth all their gadgets and gizmos. When you vanish fuses, things stop working and 'umans get super mad, see. I've seen 'oovers flying out windows, men wrestling with power cords. And you should of 'eard the lady next door, Woowee! The things she called 'er electric mixer were dark enough to curl my delicate ears – and all because I took the fuse out!"

"She'd be calling you worse things if she got hold of you, you idiot." The Jinn rolled his eyes.

"Ouch!" Marlin made a pained expression. "I'm not going back there again then."

"You're not going back in my computer again either, you ugly, walking nightmare," Kelvin told him with a finger pointed at him.

Marlin looked stunned. He furrowed his little eyebrows and scowled. "'ow dare you insult me. I is just 'aving some good clean fun with you. That's all."

"When will you learn, Marlin? People don't like troublemaking little gits. Especially when they make a person's expensive computer malfunction." The Jinn conjured a swirling portal. "Now, sod off home. I'll see you at the Tipsy Toadstool for a pint of nectar later."

Marlin hung his almost bald head and slumped at the shoulders. "I is sorry 'uman. gremlins is unable to sit still for too long. We is 'aving to tinker with things and cause trouble to be 'appy, you see."

"I understand. There are no hard feelings, mate." Kelvin put out a finger and smiled as Marlin took it in both hands and shook it.

"You is nice 'uman," he said humbly.

"Well, I do try to be nice." Kelvin became thoughtful for a moment. "You know what, Marlin. If you promise to make things work with your tinkering, instead of breaking them – you could visit from time to time."

"Really?" Marlin beamed and danced a little jig.

117

"Sure, I could use a hand repairing things now and then." Kelvin returned the smile.

"Aww, in 'e a nice 'uman, Jinn?"

"Yeah, too nice. I'd have squashed you flat if I was him," the Jinn sighed, and winked at Kelvin. "Goodbye, Marlin," he added before kicking him up the backside. The gremlin was caught unawares, the impact sent him flying through the portal.

Kelvin was sure he said something unrepeatable as he vanished but he'd never know now. "Will Marlin come back, do you think?"

"Well, he can make portals to Earth, so he might." The Jinn spread his hands as he rose into the air. "Well, your computer troubles are over, anyway."

"Affirmative. Thank you, buddy."

The Jinn snapped his fingers as his body took on a warm red glow. "Your superheroes have their heads again too."

Kelvin saw his figurines beautiful restored on the shelf. "Cheers, Jinn. I appreciate a man who repairs the damage he causes."

"Me too!" The Jinn was now hovering under the ceiling fan. "So, when you ethically hack someone, I guess you say 'sorry' afterwards do you?"

"I…" Kelvin closed his mouth. The Jinn had vanished. Kelvin smiled, shook his head and laughed. That was the strangest half-hour of his life.

About the Author

Mason Bushell is a naturalist in every way and spends much of his time in the nature reserves and woodlands by his home. His faithful dog Lucy is never too far away, especially when he is experimenting with the culinary arts. He hopes you enjoy reading his stories as much as he enjoyed writing them.

Mason's site:
https://masonsmenagerie.wordpress.com/

Other Books by Mason Bushell

A Compendium of Characters

The world of imagination is a magical place filled with fantastical stories. Inside *A Compendium of Characters* you'll be drawn into myth, legend, and mystery on every page, and across various genres. You'll meet aliens, vampires, angels, and maybe a ghost or two; discover stranded people, farmers with shotguns and people to save. There'll be romantic liaisons, fairytale frolics, and mysteries to solve!

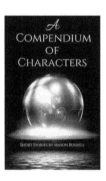

"Mason Bushell has a distinct style of writing which is light and easy to read. He knows how to build a story to create suspense and cliff hangers, and can create dark scary tension too. He creates engaging characters with depth and skilfully includes humour in dialogue. His descriptive abilities are often detailed in such a way that you wonder if he has professional knowledge of the subject, whether writing science fiction, architecture or tales-at-sea, and he does it without info dumping or showing off; it simply adds to the story and characters." (*Amazon*)

Order from Amazon:

Paperback: ISBN 979-8-618077-60-6
eBook: ASIN B0854PGWX2

Holly

Holly Ward is a natural-born mystery solver. She spends her days as a waitress in her mother's restaurant, and her spare time scuppering criminals. Trained from a young age by her Detective Grandfather, she sees all puzzles as a challenge and loves to try and work them out, leading to all sorts of mysteries and adventures.

This collection of stories is an introduction to the *Workhouse (Restaurant) Mysteries* series, and of course our cozy-mystery solver Holly: her background, her upbringing and how she came to be the crime solving sleuth she is today.

"If you like gentle Cozy Mysteries, then The Workhouse Mysteries are for you. With a restaurant as a backdrop, they tell the stories of a young 18 year old girl, Holly, who is inspired by her Detective grandfather to solve puzzles and become a sleuth."
(*Amazon*)

Order from Amazon:
eBook: ASIN B07YR38PDY

Other Publications by Chapeltown

The Basilwade Chronicles

By Dawn Knox

The Basilwade stories were originally published on the CaféLit
website, where you can access short stories that go nicely with
a cuppa. We even suggest a drink! Dawn Knox's stories
contain characters and situations that may seem a little larger
than life at first glance but we can soon see that everyone
involved is very human. And don't we all recognise the
quirkiness of village/small-town life?.

"It's been a long time since I spent so much of my time laughing
while reading a book. Endlessly inventive, crackling jokes, no two
characters alike. And every story ends, not with a cliffhanger or a
hook into the next one, but the eager need to answer the
question, 'NOW WHAT HAPPENS?'

If Basilwade doesn't actually exist somewhere, it thoroughly
deserves to!" (*Amazon*)

Order from Amazon:

Paperback: ISBN 978-1-910542-49-1
eBook: ISBN 978-1-910542-47-7

Chapeltown Books

"The Best of CaféLit" series

Each story in these little volumes is the right length and quality for enjoying as you sip the assigned drink in your favourite Creative Café. You need never feel alone again in a café. So what's the mood today? Espresso? Earl Grey tea? Hot chocolate with marshmallows? You'll find most drinks in our drinks index.

Order from Amazon:

CaféLit 2011
ISBN: 978-0-9568680-3-9 (paperback) 978-0-9568680-4-6 (ebook)
CaféLit 2012
ISBN: 978-0-9568680-8-4 (paperback) 978-0-9568680-9-1 (ebook)
CaféLit 3
ISBN: 978-1-910542-00-2 (paperback) 978-1-910542-01-9 (ebook)
CaféLit 4
ISBN: 978-1-910542-02-6 (paperback) 978-1-910542-03-3 (ebook)
CaféLit 5
ISBN: 978-1-910542-04-0 (paperback) 978-1-910542-05-7 (ebook)
CaféLit 6
ISBN: 978-1-910542-17-0 (paperback) 978-1-910542-18-7 (ebook)
CaféLit 7
ISBN: 978-1-910542-40-8 (paperback) 978-1-910542-41-5 (ebook)
CaféLit 8
ISBN: 978-1-910542-45-3 (paperback) 978-1-910542-46-0 (ebook)
CaféLit 9
ISBN: 978-1-910542-54-5 (paperback) 978-1-910542-55-2 (ebook)

Chapeltown Books